WITHDRAWN

# WHEN IMPOSSIBLE HAPPENS

# WHEN IMPOSSIBLE HAPPENS

## JANE DE SUZA

putnam

G. P. Putnam's Sons

# G. P. Putnam's Sons
An imprint of Penguin Random House LLC, New York

First published in the United States of America by G. P. Putnam's Sons,
an imprint of Penguin Random House LLC, 2023

Text copyright © 2021 by Jane De Suza
Illustrations copyright © 2023 by Chaaya Prabhat
First published by Puffin Books, Penguin Random House India, 2021

G. P. Putnam's Sons is a registered trademark of Penguin Random House LLC.
The Penguin colophon is a registered trademark of Penguin Books Limited.

Visit us online at penguinrandomhouse.com.

Library of Congress Cataloging-in-Publication Data
Names: Suza, Jane de, author.
Title: When impossible happens / Jane De Suza.
Other titles: When the world went dark
Description: New York: G. P. Putnam's Sons, 2023. | Originally published by Penguin Random House India in 2021 under title: When the world went dark. | Summary: "During the pandemic lockdown in India, almost-nine-year-old Swara's irrepressible spirit helps her come to terms with the death of her grandmother and solve a neighborhood mystery"—Provided by publisher.
Identifiers: LCCN 2022006928 (print) | LCCN 2022006929 (ebook) | ISBN 9780593530122 (hardcover) | ISBN 9780593530139 (epub) |
Subjects: CYAC: Loss—Fiction. | Grief—Fiction. | Grandmothers—Fiction. | Quarantine—Fiction. | COVID-19 Pandemic, 2020— —Fiction. | Family life—India—Fiction. | Mystery and detective stories. | LCGFT: Detective and mystery fiction. | Novels.
Classification: LCC PZ7.1.S888 Wh 2023 (print) | LCC PZ7.1.S888 (ebook) | DDC [Fic]—dc23
LC record available at https://lccn.loc.gov/2022006928
LC ebook record available at https://lccn.loc.gov/2022006929

Printed in the United States of America

ISBN 9780593530122
1st Printing

LSCH

Design by Eileen Savage. Text set in Dante MT Pro.

*If you've lost someone you love,*

*and ask Why Me?*

*And sometimes,*

*Why Not Me?*

# Meet my family and friends

**Swara** • Me. Almost nine years old. Star of the story.

**Amma** • Mother

**Appa** • Father

**Amma and Appa** • Mother and Father—or, when they act like two fused Lego blocks, **Amma-Appa**

**Rishi** • Brother who is older and acts V. Busy and V. Bossy

**Pitter Paati (PP)** • Grandmother (mother's mother) and favoritest person ever

**Thaatha** • Grandfather (mother's father)

**Anand Maama** • Uncle (mother's brother), with whom my grandparents live

**Maami** • Aunt, Anand Maama's wife

**Kriti and Kolam** • Four-year-old twin cousins, who are V. Annoying

**Madurai Paati** • Grandmother (father's mother), who lives in Madurai

**Ruth** • Across-the-landing neighbor, maybe best friend, and (she made me add this) founder of her own hairbrush news channel

**Deborah (Debbie)** • Ruth's older sister and secret someone of secret someone else

**Zarir** • Double friend (from school and apartment building)

**Dr. Mariyam Aunty** • Zarir's mother and a doctor

**Dr. Ansari** • Zarir's father and a doctor who is Not. A. Fool.

**Abba** • What Zarir calls his father

**Nina Miss** • Teacher

**Govind Uncle** • Building security guard, who thinks I'm still a baby

**Akka** • What I call our maid out of respect (it means older sister)

**Viru** • Friend and neighbor

**Harsha and Uttara** • Detective squad minions

**Muffet** • My newest friend, who is shhhh!

# When the World Went Dark

The times were dark, alarming, threatening. Clouds of fear kept people bolted and barred into their own homes. You couldn't open a window to draw in a deep breath. You couldn't trust anything that anyone else had touched. In fact, if you remember, you couldn't even put a toe out of your front door.

Swara should know because she tested it out.

Ruth was the one who'd thrown her the challenge. She claimed to be her best friend, although you might doubt it after this. They lived in apartments opposite each other and often they sat cross-legged on their doormats and chatted, yelling to and fro. It was Ruth who said, "Swara, you cannot put even a toe out of your door."

Swara scoffed at this. "Why? What if I do?"

"Try and see. It is banned! There is a high-tech app that will make your toe shrivel up and fall off."

If you've been almost nine, like Swara was, you know what absolutely had to be done if such an outrageous challenge was thrown down. Swara, quite naturally, had to still her beating heart, hold her breath, kick off her slipper, and wiggle her big toe an inch out of her open door. It did not fall off and land on the doormat. It stayed firmly on her foot.

"You are full of lies, Ruth!"

"I am not. I am the Ruth, the whole Ruth, and nothing but the—"

"Fine, but my toe is fine too. It is my toe, the whole toe, and nothing but the toe."

"It will not be for long. Keep watching it. Over the days, it will turn red, purple, black, and then fall right off. Just you wait."

Swara retreated, scared. And began to watch the toe for signs.

The times were like that, as we've mentioned. Dark, alarming, threatening times.

And then, of course, school was closed—out of the blue! No waking up to a screaming alarm clock, or drinking milk while sleepwalking, or pulling on the uniform and buttoning it wrong, or running down to catch the yellow school bus and missing the favorite seat.

Like most kids, Swara spent the first week playing, eating, and sleeping and, like most kids, got fed up with it all. Nothing fun was on the Allowed List. No playing downstairs, no eating out, no meeting friends. To add to her dismay, her toe sported a smallish reddish spot one morning, which turned her as white as a sheet (just a saying). She held her toe in one hand and hopped over to Appa, who examined it and opined that it was a harmless insect bite and would disappear soon.

"My toe? My toe will disappear?"

"No, Swara, the red spot will disappear," her father said.

What was high up on the Rotten List was that she couldn't visit her favorite person in the world, her paati. Not Madurai Paati, her father's mother, but Pitter Paati, her mother's mother, who lived on the outskirts of Bengaluru. In the same city and not visitable! V. Stupid (Very Stupid)! Everyone was locked down—Pitter Paati; her grandpa, Thaatha; her uncle and aunt, whom she called Anand Maama and Maami; and the twins (her V. Annoying cousins). The whole city was locked into their houses.

The whole world too, from what the TV showed. You could see people in Italy singing and waving while hanging over their balconies. Swara made a point of letting Ruth know that no one's arms were turning purple, shriveling up, and falling off.

She video called Pitter Paati many times a day, to show her a new poem, the suspicious red-spotted toe, the view of no one on the streets outside, a line of ants creeping toward the dustbin, her fake mustache, anything actually. PP was always interested in whatever Swara was up to.

☆ ☆ ☆

You had better know some more about Pitter Paati. It's essential that you do, because you may see then why Swara wouldn't believe what happened next.

In fact, if you peek through Swara's V. Private

diary—which is an invasion of privacy—you'll find an old poem she began.

> Pitter Paati was full of fun.
> She brought me up from when I was one.
> Because Amma-Appa went to office.

She'd stopped rhyming because nothing rhymed with *office* or with what came next, except *muzzles* . . .

> She was full of games and puzzles (see?)
> And she loved crime thrillers
> and detective fiction (still no rhymes).
> And we sat for hours while she acted
> out her favorite detective stories starring
> Feluda, Karamchand, and, most of all, Miss
> Marple, who she said was an old woman
> like her and smarter than everyone, like
> her. She called me her Little Miss Marple.

"You got it wrong, Pitter Paati," Swara objected when she was little. (As she would remind you, she was old now—almost nine.) "It's Little Miss Muffet."

"Did she also solve murder mysteries?"

Swara thought it over. "No. She wasn't brave. She ran away from a tuffet because of a spider."

"That's it, then, you are too brave to be sitting on a tuffet, whatever that is . . . or to be afraid of the lovely species around it."

"I don't think a tuffet is an actual stool thing; I think they couldn't rhyme either."

Thereafter, PP called Swara Little Miss Marple, but because she was so tiny then, it seemed more appropriate to call her Little Miss Marble. After all, Swara had called her grandma Pitter Paati for years, though it meant nothing and just conjured up the sound of rain. Special people, after all, deserve special code names.

It's V. Important that you understand all this about Pitter Paati, because you will then understand that she wouldn't just disappear one day without telling Swara.

Would she?

A V. Ridiculous thought, really!

A couple of days into the lockdown, Pitter Paati fell sick. She often fell sick. She would sing songs of rhyming complaints featuring her chest pain, migraine, and forgetful brain. She had a handful of colorful tablets on her bedside table, which were to be taken with every meal. This time, Anand Maama said, it was more serious. Neither her fever nor her cough would go away.

Amma looked worried, so Swara told her not to worry; she'd make PP a fantastic Get Well Soon card. These fantastic cards had always worked in the past, and she'd Gotten Well Soon as ordered. In fact, Pitter Paati had insisted that it was the cards and not the medicine that had worked miracles.

Swara went at it with military discipline. She drew one card a day, with rainbows and puppies (there was no harm in hinting to Amma-Appa just how much she wanted a puppy). Rishi said that her puppy looked like a pig. She told Rishi that he was a pig. That's the kind of thing you could tell your bothersome brother, even if he was many years older. Honestly, she wouldn't have minded a pig either. She wouldn't share it with Rishi, though.

Her cards had long poems (because PP didn't mind that she couldn't rhyme), which she would show and read out to Pitter Paati over video calls. This time, however, Pitter Paati seemed to always be in bed, even in the middle of the morning, when she had usually been such a fizzy-busy person. She kept coughing over the calls, so Swara had to stop (reading) and continue when Pitter Paati stopped (coughing).

Swara regaled her grandmother with her own made-up detective stories starring Miss Marble and her pig-puppy. She sang for her on video calls. She complained about Ruth and Rishi.

One morning later that week, Anand Maama said Pitter Paati couldn't take her call because she was overly tired.

Swara was V. Angry with her uncle, but he insisted that Pitter Paati was too sick. He said that they were concerned she could have caught the virus because some visitors earlier had tested positive, so she needed to go to the hospital, and they were taking her right then. He told her not to worry, as the doctors were excellent and would cure her soon.

On the TV news, they told everyone to wear masks to save themselves.

Of course! That was the only thing missing, the

only thing Swara hadn't done till then. She told Amma the next day that she would make a mask to save Pitter Paati. Appa helped her make it, and Swara drew a big smiley face on the front and a big red heart around that.

"Why have you added this little dot?" her father asked.

"It's me. Little Miss Marble. You won't get it. It's a secret Pitter Paati and I have." She folded the mask and gave it to Appa, who promised that Swara's mother would drive over and give it to PP that very evening. Amma had gotten herself a pass to travel. She could step outside the house without risking her toes falling off.

Swara tried waiting up for Amma's return, but when she got back home, it was very late, and the almost-nine-year-old had fallen asleep at the dining table (and was magically carried over to her bed, as usual).

Early the next morning, when she bounded out, Amma, Appa, and Rishi were gathered around the dining table. Swara went straight to the point. "Did you give Pitter Paati my mask?"

No one said anything. No one looked at her.

"Amma?" She tugged at her mother's sleeve, noticing that it was the same kurta she'd had on the previous night. "What did Pitter Paati say? Did she wear my mask? Did she notice Little Miss Marble on it?" Then, as a big lump knotted in her stomach, she demanded more frantically, "Amma! When are the excellent doctors sending her home?"

Amma put her face into her hands then. Appa pulled Swara over, cupped her face, and said softly, "There's something you have to know, Swara."

"No. Let Pitter Paati tell me. When is she coming home?"

"Pitter Paati is not coming home, Swara. She's gone."

V. Ridiculous! The things grown-ups say sometimes.

"Where did she go?" Swara asked. Where else could you go from a hospital if not home? The lump grew heavier because she was old enough to guess. Almost nine.

"She caught the virus. Her heart was too weak. I'm sorry, Baby."

"I am not a baby. Her heart isn't weak. She has the strongest, biggest, kindest heart ever."

They sat silently. The big fat liars. All of them. And it wasn't even the first of April.

"Where did she go?" she screamed and screamed at them.

# The Making of a Detective

Then the calls began. Almost nonstop. On Amma's phone, on Appa's phone, on the landline. Amma held up her hand to wave away many of them. No, she didn't want to talk. Then they'd ask to speak to Rishi and then to Swara.

*Be strong, Swara.*

*You must move on now. Don't look back.*

*You must act like a big girl now.* (She was almost nine, she'd reply first and later realize that they weren't interested in what she had to say, not really, not like Pitter Paati was.)

*You must be strong for your mother.*

*This too shall pass.* (Said another uncle, who always

called to report about his kidney stones and when they had passed.)

*Your grandmother would have wanted you to carry on.*

*She was a wonderful lady.*

*Remember, Swara, we are with you.* (They were not; they were in lockdown elsewhere.)

They were all liars. Idiots. Fools. Swara's grandfather loved to use the word *fools*. Thaatha would read the newspaper and look up and say, "Fools!" Or he'd watch politicians give speeches on TV and say, "Fools!" Even when there were people jogging in the park on a sunny or rainy day, he'd say, "Fools!"

Thaatha didn't call. He didn't want to speak to anyone either. Swara was made to speak to the twins, though, her V. Annoying cousins who lived with Pitter Paati. Wasn't it unfair that Kriti and Kolam got to spend all that time with her when Swara was the one who tried so hard to make her Get Well Soon? Additionally, they were four-year-olds, so they could not even speak coherently. It was an insult to her dignity to have to talk to them about anything as important as this. She tried putting up her hand too, saying,

"I don't want to speak." But of course she was made to. Everyone bosses around an almost-nine-year-old.

"Hello," she said, going straight to the point. "I hope you don't believe that Paati has gone off, because she hasn't."

"My tooth fell off," Kolam said.

"Did you get a puppy?" asked Kriti.

"No." Swara kept the conversation serious like any older cousin should. "Look, you have to help me. Everyone is telling lies. Paati has not . . . not . . . She's just not gone off like they say, okay? Will you help me search for her?"

"She's gone. To the hospital."

Swara dropped her voice to a whisper. "She must have left clues. Will you go look under her pillow?"

"I have to wash hands," Kolam complained.

"I cannot go swim," Kriti complained.

"You got a puppy?" Kolam asked.

Fools! She disconnected the call.

She didn't mind taking Zarir's call. Zarir was her double friend—from school and from their building. His father was a doctor in the hospital, and he said he'd heard about her grandmother.

"Will you ask your doctor father where she's gone?" she asked him with hope in her heart.

"H-huh? Where?" Zarir stuttered and muttered, and she got mad at him. She had to get mad at someone. She couldn't keep hoping and then hitting a dead end each time.

"Your father is a useless doctor if he can't even get people well soon, and it is all his fault that everyone is getting sick and not getting better. If he really was an excellent doctor, he could make them Get Well Soon."

Zarir screamed back. Not nice words.

"Fool!" she shouted. "You are a fool. Your father is a fool doctor. His hospital is a fool hospital."

Zarir's mother came on the call then. Dr. Mariyam Aunty was a doctor too, the kind who talks to you to treat you. "Swara, dear one"—*dear one* was usually followed by unhelpful advice, Little Miss Marble thought—"why don't you write a letter to your grandmother? Tell her everything you want to. It may help you."

"Thank you very much for calling. Have a good day. Press the red icon to disconnect." Swara congratulated herself on being formal and polite.

The other calls kept coming in.

What she had to do: Be brave. Be strong. Be positive.

What she could not do: Be sad. Cry. Think of the past.

Fools!

She got so angry that tears began to prick her eyelids, but of course, she couldn't cry because that would mean she believed what they said about Pitter Paati. And it was V. Obviously not true.

Pitter Paati wouldn't just leave her and go, without even telling her where. It was V. Ridiculous. V. Impossible! She wouldn't do that. The detective stories fan that she was, the least she would have done was to leave Swara clues.

That was it: clues that no one was smart enough to find, except Little Miss Marble. She would bring back her favorite person in the world.

☆ ☆ ☆

It became increasingly evident to Swara that all the grown-ups knew nothing. They were all wrong. Pitter Paati was the one exception. She knew everything. She had answers to all questions, like *Do ducks and pelicans speak the same language? Would ostriches have a different accent maybe?*

And then she just went off with all her answers—???

Obviously not. V. Ridiculous! V. Rubbish!

PP was just setting up a real-life mystery. She had, without a doubt, scattered clues about how to find her again. And wouldn't they all look stupid when Swara found her?

Quite possibly, she would even be rewarded then. Perhaps even with a puppy.

The hunt commenced on the balcony. Swara first looked at PP's favorite rocking chair, under all those cushions. Then the shelf PP used when she came over, which was stuffed with her wool and knitting needles and books. Then in that corner in the kitchen cabinet, where she hid her sweets behind her medicine bottles to fool Amma. (She didn't fool Amma. No one could fool Amma.)

Swara searched every nook and cranny of the house. She found silver cobwebs behind the sofas, a coin, a few pens, the bill that Appa lost, a slice of bread covered in green fungus.

Exhausted by the end of the day, Swara sulked;

it was just like Pitter Paati to make this mystery V. Exceptionally Tough. And then it struck her. Of course! V. Obvious! She would have hidden it in something she'd made especially for her Little Miss Marble. Like that doll she'd knitted.

Where had it gone?

Swara drove herself into a frenzy. She would not eat till she'd found it. The world would not spin till she'd found it.

What made it a wee bit more painful was that Swara remembered that she hadn't liked the doll when PP had placed it into her hands. It looked too . . . non-tech. It had none of the superpowers that her action heroes had. Swara didn't even play with dolls usually, and to make it worse, this one had button eyes and orange wool skin.

That's how she remembered where it was. It also made her feel like a terrible, hateful human being. She'd thrown it as far and as high as she could. And it had landed on top of the bookshelf, right on top, where no one dusted.

Swara jumped on the bed. She couldn't reach the

doll. She put her chair on the bed, jumped on the chair, and then fell off.

Rishi dashed in, shouting, "What is that noise you're making, Dumbo? Some of us are trying to study."

A translation for those of you who haven't been in sibling wars lately:

Dumbo = Swara. Some of us = Rishi.

Swara noted that he showed no sympathy for his little sister, who lay collapsed on the bed. But then, that's what terrible, hateful human beings deserve!

"Pitter Paati's doll is up there. Can you get it for me?"

"Why should I?"

"Please." She never said "please" to him. This was a fact that Appa was in the dark about. He thought both his children had "exceptional" manners. They'd overheard him bragging to someone on the phone. In reality, they were rarely polite to each other when no one else was listening. It didn't mean they didn't love each other; it was actually quite the opposite. It meant they did—they loved each other so much that they could say whatever they wanted to. It's strange how we sometimes treat those we love the most.

Here's proof. "Some of us" rescued "Dumbo's" doll. In simpler terms, Rishi jumped up and pulled the doll by its one leg that was sticking out. It was covered in dust. Swara shook it and patted it down. Then she laid it on the bed, carefully looking all over its orange wool skin for a clue.

Pitter Paati was really smart. The clue would be cleverly hidden inside.

She poked at it gingerly. She rolled its limbs around. She then pulled out its button eyes, getting slightly frantic. Nothing hidden under them.

Desperate by then, she cut a hole in its lumpy middle. She pushed her fingers in and began to yank out its stuffing.

Socks!

Pitter Paati had stuffed it with old socks. She recognized school socks where the elastic bands had worn off. She recognized the non-matching single socks Appa always complained about. She recognized Thaatha's woolen socks through which his big toes stuck out.

She shook out the socks. Each one.

No clues.

She looked at the sad orange doll, thin and flat with no insides. She felt like the sad orange doll, thin and flat with no insides.

She curled up on her bed, head buried in the socks. For a long, long time.

☆ ☆ ☆

Later, she told Ruth about it all. "Throw over the doll and socks," Ruth said. "My mom is the world's best knitter." Swara knew that Pitter Paati was, but she let it go. Out of her open door, she threw the doll, socks, buttons . . . They ended up in the middle of the landing, and Ruth crawled out, gathered them up, and took them in. She didn't seem to mind that her arms would shrivel and fall off.

That's what friends are like.

Ruth's mom heard the story (and that Ruth added lots to it is something we can all be certain about). She immediately left her own work to sew the knitted doll together, with its socks stuffed back in. Ruth made sure she didn't leave out a single one.

Swara was happy. If her knitted doll could Get Well Soon, Pitter Paati would most definitely too. Proof!

Wait a minute. Happy? Happy when PP was nowhere in sight? How could she ever be happy? Huh! She was not happy. She was sorry she'd even thought of being happy. She hoped that Pitter Paati wouldn't think it meant that she'd forgotten about her. She announced loudly and clearly to no one in particular that she would never be happy again till she'd found her.

# After Fox Clues, Fox Bags

It's difficult to keep believing in something if everyone around you believes in the opposite. Take the next day, for example. Amma and Appa had got a special pass to go out, they said, for Paati's last rites memorial.

"What will you write? In these last writes?" Swara asked them.

When no one answered, she declared, "There is no need for 'last' anything for Pitter Paati. She is coming back."

Swara suspected it was a ruse. They were going off somewhere else without her.

She resumed her detective work on the sly. For instance, when Amma went in for a shower, she

quickly rifled through her big brown fox leather bag.
When Swara had first learned of it, she had been ready
to set up a howl about the poor fox, but Amma had
quickly shown Swara the label that said *faux leather.*
Rishi had explained that meant that it wasn't actually
from a fox or any other animal. Although Rishi, as it
has been seen before, could not be trusted.

Get this: She found her mask among the many
things stuffed into Amma's bag. The mask she'd
painted on for Pitter Paati. Amma hadn't given it to
her at all. *She* had stopped Swara from saving PP.

She was overwhelmed with indignation, quite
understandably. Nevertheless, like good detectives
who stand unblinking, whether they are confront-
ing murderers or just liars like her mother . . . Swara
stayed calm.

Amma came out dressed all in white, with a red
face. Her eyes were blurry red, her nose was chili red,
and her cheeks looked like apples.

Appa looked around helplessly and finally said,
"Swara, would you like to write a little song or note to
remember Paati by? We can read it out at the ceremony."

Swara stayed calm and said nothing.

"Oh, come on, Swara, don't sulk. This is your last chance," said Rishi from the couch. Another "last" word? She added Rishi to her Suspects of the Day List.

"Okay, then, tell her I know what no one else knows," Swara said mysteriously. She stuffed the mask into the pocket of her shorts and stomped off.

Appa said, "Look, Baby, we may be able to bring Thaatha home. That would be nice, wouldn't it? It would help you both to talk about Paati. You should be able to talk about it openly. That will make you feel better."

Grown-ups, grown-ups! They try to help, but they end up saying the wrong things. That only made Swara feel ten times more rotten.

Thaatha wasn't Pitter Paati. Thaatha was always reading books or newspapers in the hope of finding more fools. He didn't know how to escape from disguised criminals or talk in alien sign language.

And besides, if her grandfather came over to stay, she'd have to give up her room and go squeeze herself between Amma-Appa like a baby. Which one couldn't do when one was almost nine. But most importantly, Thaatha always came with Pitter Paati. It was a rule! V. Unbreakable rule! So if he came alone, it would only make her miss Pitter Paati more.

Not feeling glad about Thaatha coming over made her feel rottener than rottenest—whatever that was.

She didn't bother responding to Appa's plea for her last writes.

She didn't hug red-faced Amma, who was holding out her arms.

She didn't even look at Rishi, who had to stay home to babysit her and shoot her resentful looks.

Fools!

☆ ☆ ☆

Much later, sitting all alone, looking out of the window, Swara wondered afresh why she had not been taken to visit Pitter Paati. To the hospital earlier. To this ceremony now. Was it her fault that Pitter Paati had disappeared? Was she to blame in some way? Was that why they hadn't given her the Get Well Soon mask? Was that why PP said she was too tired to take her video calls?

Was Pitter Paati angry with her? What had she done wrong? Had she not tried hard enough? Had she not been good enough? Had she pestered PP too often? Was this all somehow her fault?

☆ ☆ ☆

Swara took out her V. Secret diary. She ran her palm along a blank page, and she decided, as Appa had told her, to write down her feelings. Only, she didn't know what her feelings were or where to start.

She didn't know whom to be angry with. Whom to blame. Why she was sad. Why she felt guilty. How to make sense of the confusion. Why she felt abandoned by her favorite person in the world. Why she felt useless for not doing something more.

Swara didn't realize that that was exactly what she could have written down.

Perhaps almost-nines aren't old enough to know these things? Then what age is?

The questions were bouncing around in her head when someone else's voice sliced into the silence. Rishi was talking to a friend on his phone in his room. She wondered why he could talk to other people but not to his own sister. She heard him mention a puppy. She thought that was V. Selfish of him because she was the one who wanted a puppy. V. Inconsiderate! She took all the feelings she couldn't write about and stacked them into a huge Lego tower of anger against the V. Annoying Rishi.

## Reasons to Hate Rishi:

1. He is almost seventeen. He shows off that he is older. Like ALL the time. He thinks that almost nine is still a baby.

2. He calls me Boondi Ladoo. Not because it's a nice, golden, sweet treat, but because it's round. Just because I was a chubby baby. V. Rude!

3. He does not answer my questions seriously. He told me that papaya was poisonous (it's V. Delicious).

4. He studies all day. He is only worried about himself, his stupid exams next year, and his stupider college admission after that.

5. He doesn't play Ludo or Monopoly with me anymore.

6. He is talking to his friends like life is normal. And it is NOT!!! Nothing is normal.

7. Most of all because Pitter Paati's gone and . . .

8. He is not crying!

Swara walked out of her room and told him,

"Boys don't cry. But real men cry. I saw it in a TV commercial."

She stomped back in again and slammed her door shut. She thought it would make her feel smart and good about herself.

It didn't.

☆ ☆ ☆

If she couldn't write her fool feelings in her fool diary, there was no harm in writing to Pitter Paati like Dr. Mariyam Aunty had said, right? After much thought and six and a half attempts (the half attempt was because her pen made a hole through the paper), Swara tore up the long letters and wrote a short one.

She pushed it under the cushions on Pitter Paati's favorite rocking chair on the balcony. The chair sagged in the middle, but PP had enjoyed sitting on it, propped up among the many cushions. Swara used to sit beside her, on the floor, dangling her legs through the lattice grille of the railing. That was where they talked and solved crimes together, coming ably to the assistance of the famous private investigator Feluda and his crew. For want of a better idea,

Swara decided to hide the letter there until she found a way to get it to PP.

> Dear Pitter Paati,
>
> I know that you know that I know you're out there somewhere. I just don't know where. Send me clues. V. Soon please. Thank you.
>
> I love you best in the world. Everyone else is being a fool!!!
>
> Your Little Miss Marble

# Crime Reporters Live

One of Swara's favorite stories was that of a man who couldn't move. Wait, there's more. This man solved a murder mystery while confined to his bed, just by looking out of his window. The story was told, of course, by You-Know-Who.

Fascinated by that story, she developed a strong attachment to her own bedroom window during the lockdown. It gave her time to think about PP and to dream up scenarios where she was swashbuckling her way through detective work.

She spent most nights after dinner curled up on her chair, staring out of her window. The view wasn't exactly dark and mysterious. Their building overlooked other buildings in the apartment complex.

Since they were on the second floor, it offered a view largely of the other tall towers.

At night, she could see things happening inside different apartments, and she tried to figure out if anyone was stealing, fighting, or generally being criminal. The neighbors, however, turned out to be boring. Most windows showed people eating or watching TV or, even more boring, eating while watching TV. No one did anything suspicious. Rishi told her to stop being gory. She told him she was stopping others from being gory. He said she was after fame and gory. And laughed at his own fool joke. (To add to the Reasons to Hate Rishi List.)

If she looked to the right, she could see the main gate and security cabin diagonally below them, and then the street outside. Across the street were three-story buildings with all kinds of shops piled up. Even duller! The street was usually full of cars whizzing past, squeezing into other lanes when their own lane was jammed, bikes squeezing between cars, people squeezing between bikes. Nothing worth a good detective's time—even during regular times, that is.

During the lockdown, it was positively sleep-inducing. Quiet, empty streets. No buses. No trucks. Just the odd car or bike (just a saying—the cars were normal, not odd). All the shops were closed, except for the pharmacy. She stared so long at the large green first aid cross on the glass pane of the pharmacy that she soon saw green crosses all over. No one was acting remotely criminal in there either.

## MAP (Appa helped me draw this)

1. Where I watch everything happen
2. Govind Uncle's security cabin
3. Gate
4. Windows of other apartments where Nothing Exciting Happens. Yawn!
5. Main street outside
6. Boring shops . . . Only the pharmacy with a big green cross is open.
7. Where I saw the . . . Wait for it to happen!
8. The moon, which sends no messages. V. Useless moon. It ends here!

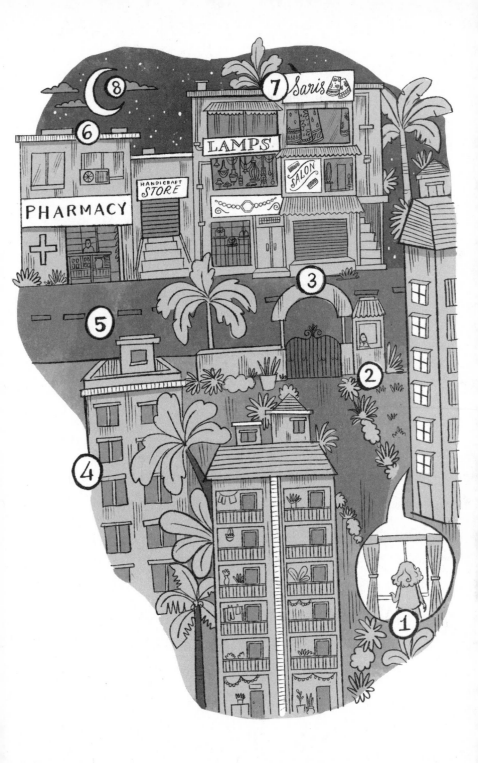

One night in particular, she stared gloomily at the pharmacy as it was being shuttered for the night, the manager squatting to secure the locks at the bottom. He then kicked his motorbike to life and rode off. She yawned. A police motorcycle rode past. She was about to give up on crime spotting when something stopped her.

Another motorbike, with its headlights off, had crawled to a stop. She initially thought it was going to the pharmacy and felt sad because it was closed and the people would not get medicines for their poisoned relatives (the ongoing story in her mind). It stopped at the pharmacy all right, but then two men got off and walked quickly to the building three shopfronts away. There was something in the way they walked, hunched over and sneaking glances over their shoulders, that got Swara interested. They fiddled with what she presumed was the lock, opened the door that led to the staircase of the building, and disappeared.

After a while, Swara spotted lights flickering inside the shop on the third floor. That was a sari shop. She knew what every shop sold. What were they doing in a sari shop during the lockdown, and at night? You were only allowed out to buy essential goods.

Surely saris were not essential goods?

She called Zarir, forgetting it was late at night and forgetting that they had been screaming not-so-nice words at each other, which demanded a couple of days of Not Talking. He had clearly not forgotten, because he was still sulking.

"Are saris essential goods?" Swara never bothered with niceties like Hello and How Are You and other things you need to start putting into practice when you're past almost nine.

"Maybe if you ate them and choked, Swara. I don't care."

"Huh? Oh, are you still mad about what I said about your fool doctor father?"

"He is not a fool!"

Swara stuttered, "N-no, I mean, I said it, but I mean, I didn't mean . . ." She thought of all the excuses she could come up with. But in the end, there was just one thing to say and she said it. "Zarir, I'm sorry."

"Say you were wrong."

"I was wrong. I was."

And that was that! They continued from there.

Zarir said, "Let's see. Maybe you could make masks out of saris? Masks are essential goods. Abba told me."

Oh! The two men were not criminals, they were do-gooders who were making masks out of saris in the middle of the night. They were quite the opposite of evil, V. Noble, in fact. Swara felt V. Stupid.

She was still determined to be on Not Talking terms with all doctors, of course. But she and Zarir went back to talking again.

☆ ☆ ☆

Amma was not really crying.

She was not really crying in the kitchen. "I'm not really crying. It's the smoke," she said.

She was not really crying in the dining room. "It's the chilies in the curry," she said.

She was not really crying in the bathroom. "Soap in my eyes," she said.

She was not really crying when looking through old photo albums. "Just dust," she said.

Swara said, "You can Not Really Cry on my shoulder."

Amma was sitting on her bed, surrounded by dusty albums. She put an arm around Swara, who stood beside the bed, and buried her face into her daughter's sweater.

Amma was not really crying on her shoulder. "It's just an allergy to your woolen sweater," she said.

Swara tried to be strong for her but saw that she had been looking at the photo of Pitter Paati as a happy young woman on a happy new bicycle. A single tear, quite without her permission, rolled down Swara's cheek and chin and dropped onto Amma's head, along the parting in her hair.

"I'm not really crying. It's your hair tickling my nose," Swara whispered. Then she stopped. "No. I am really crying. It's Pitter Paati," she said.

"Yes, it's Pitter Paati," Amma said.

☆ ☆ ☆

"Reporting from Petunia Tower, 2C and 2D. This is the Ruth of the Matter, brought to you live."

"What about me?" Swara asked, annoyed. "I'm reporting too."

Ruth and Swara were sitting just inside their doorways, talking across the hall as usual. Ruth had a hairbrush in her hand, which she wielded like a mic.

"Okay, then. We take you to our field reporter, Swara, now. Over to you, Swara, what is the situation on the ground?"

"Erm. It looks dirty. Now that Akka isn't allowed to come in, no one mops it daily." She looked around at the floor. Their maid was also locked into her own house far away.

Ruth hissed, "On the ground doesn't mean *on the ground*. It means everywhere else."

"Oh." Swara settled into the news report then. "There were strange happenings last night, spotted by Swara, the ground reporter, on the ground across the street, on the ground of the shop on the third floor." It was getting confusing. "There were lights flickering on and off in the sari shop, where two men were making masks out of the saris."

"Were they making supervillain masks or robber masks?" Ruth asked.

"No. I mean, just those masks that everyone should wear now. The good kind of masks, you know."

"And why is that a crime, ground reporter from the shop on the third floor, Miss Swara?"

She was quite fed up with Ruth. Just because she was a year older, she threw her weight around. (Just a saying, because apparently you cannot throw your weight off, no matter how hard you try, Amma kept complaining.) "Well, why don't you tell me if you have any more criminal news to report, then, Miss Ruth Who Doesn't Matter at All?"

Ruth held out her pretend mic. "Ruth of the Matter will now report on the global scene."

"From the ground or the air? How will you be global when you are in lockdown?"

"I have my sources," Ruth continued mysteriously. "Globally, millions are infected, millions are dying. There are people who have no homes and are living on the streets. They have no food, no water. They have no trains or planes. They have no jobs. They have no exams, which got canceled. The virus is the biggest thing that ever shook the world."

Swara protested. This was not the truth at all. "It is the smallest. It is microscopic!"

"I heard the TV. The economies are crashing. The markets are crashing too, they said."

The girls both sat lost in thought, images of market roofs crashing down on onions and cabbages filling their minds.

"Why are the markets crashing?" Swara finally had to ask.

Ruth drew imaginary lines in the air. "I present here some graphs. See the red line going up? That is the growing virus. See the red arrows going down? Those are the markets crashing."

Ruth covered her hairbrush-mic. "No one will have money ever again. My parents can't talk about anything else. Really. I get scared. Debbie's company has started layoffs already."

Deborah was Ruth's older sister, whom Rishi liked, and not like an older sister either. Only Swara knew this. She'd found out by accident and blackmailed him whenever it suited her.

"Why is her company starting those? Aren't those the basketball things?"

"Those are *layups*. *Layoffs* mean they will fire her. I don't know how to make them all feel better. And they don't even talk to me properly because I'm a kid."

The reporters on the ground sat on the ground, feeling gloomy, anxious, confused.

Swara finally said, "Me too. No one."

Except You-Know-Who.

# The Biggest Fear

I want to show you something, Swara," Amma said,
and that, as any almost-nine-year-old knows, is adult
doublespeak. It could mean cute-animal-videos stuff
or teacher's-scary-remarks stuff.

It started positively enough. Amma got Swara to
sit cross-legged on her bed, settled into a cuddle, then
opened up a discussion thread on her computer. It was
from the apartment complex chat group. Apparently,
there was news that the sari shop across the street was
donating saris to make masks. And the residents in all
of the buildings were getting signatures of volunteers
who were willing to make masks at home. This noble
initiative had gotten thirty-one enthusiastic people

signed up already. The only problem was that it was giving Swara a tummy ache.

Amma said, "Swara, do you know who started this news?"

Swara said, "Must have been Ruth or her sister or her mother or Zarir or his mother or his doctor father. They need masks, right—doctors?"

Amma continued gently, "And who do you think told them first?"

Amma scrolled to the beginning of the chat thread. It said that Young Health Warrior Swara from Petunia, 2C, had reported the sari shop's project. "Is that true, Swara?"

"No." Swara looked up at the ceiling. It made it easier to imagine thrashing Ruth or Zarir for blabbing in some not-so-distant future. "It could be true. Or not. I don't know."

"Swara, I want you to text from my phone and tell the neighbors that you don't know anything about the sari shop. And that you started the rumor. I don't want everyone to waste their time."

"You do it."

"I could. But I'd like you to take responsibility."

"Could I take responsibility some other time, please?"

"Or you could turn a mistake into something brave, right? It's up to you," Amma said.

When put like that, it made sense. In fact, she'd do something braver and go thrash Zarir AND Ruth later, Swara promised herself.

She typed this out:

It was My Mistake. The Sari shop is Not making masks. I don't know what it is making!!!! Please don't make masks too. I am Sorry.
—Young Health Warrior Swara from Petunia, 2C

Amma quickly added a message saying:

Please do continue to make masks. Just not from saris from the shop as my daughter suggested. Thanks. 😊

She had added a smiley, though she wasn't smiling. Swara made a mental note: While texting, it was easy to say what you didn't feel. The whole world was texting. Soon, no one would know what anyone else really felt.

Amma, for example, was feeling miserable and stressed (which Swara had just added to) but was still sending out smileys.

☆ ☆ ☆

Back at the window at night. Staring at the moon. Pitter Paati had said long ago that if Swara couldn't be with her, or see her or phone her, she should just talk to the moon, and PP would send answers back through the moon. That was when she was almost five. Did it still work when she was almost nine?

"Send me a clue, Pitter Paati, about where you are and what I should do," Swara whispered. Then she added, "Or if you know anything about the criminals in the sari shop."

There were lights flashing in the sari shop: dim lights at times, like from a phone screen; at other times, brighter lights, like from a flashlight; and on occasion, even brighter lights, like sparks from Diwali sparklers.

At some point, she became aware of another light. From the left—in fact, from one of the towers in her apartment complex. Most homes were dark, except the few lit rooms of people watching TV. But there! One couldn't mistake it. A single light flashing on. Off. Slowly. Then faster. OMG, Pitter Paati was actually sending clues. But what did they mean?

Was that Morse code? Swara didn't know Morse code. Why hadn't she ever learned Morse code? There she was learning useless things like synonyms and antonyms when she should have been learning Morse code all along.

She stared at the blinking light, gulping, heart hammering. This was the stuff that mysteries were made of. She absolutely had to tell Ruth or Zarir or . . . wait a minute! Or Viru! That was Viru's apartment. Magnolia Tower, 4D.

On cue, she saw his head pop into the window frame, then fall back laughing. The light stayed on. He had been flicking his study lamp on and off.

She flicked her own study lamp back at him.

He then shook his shoulders in bhangra style and threw his arms in the air, pointing his fingers upward, and began to dance. She did her best to copy him but couldn't do bhangra like he could. Her shoulders weren't as obedient.

So she changed tack. She struck a few basic poses she'd learned in classical dance class and upped the level when Viru tried to copy them.

After a few minutes of this, the two figures in the little lit windows collapsed, laughing.

Viru then picked up his cricket bat and took a few swings, which could only mean (to someone with a vivid imagination, which Swara had, without a doubt) that he was fencing. She followed suit with her badminton racket, twirling it around her head like in the story she'd read about Jhansi ki Rani.

Viru, not to be outdone, twirled his bat higher and faster.

This is when, unplanned by either, the real drama began. Because, all of a sudden, Viru's light went out and the sound of a crash carried across the towers and the lawns between them. Many heads appeared in many windows, straining to catch some of the excitement.

Viru's room light snapped on. His mom, dad,

grandfather, and brother all stood over him, their hands on their hips. His study lamp had probably crashed, and Swara could only imagine the excuses he'd have to cook up to explain. She shrank away from her window for a while. Her sari/mask commotion was still fresh, and the blame for this couldn't be added to that.

She wasn't sure what clues Pitter Paati thought she was sending over—she'd always had a mischievous sense of humor.

Or. Or. Or was it just punishment for dancing around and being silly when PP had disappeared and Swara ought to be feeling sad instead? No more dancing! No more acting silly! Fool Viru!

She promised not to get distracted again.

She promised to stare at the moon instead.

To stop dancing. To stop yawning.

To wait for clues.

To wait for Pitter Paati's messages even when her eyes were closing.

She sat staring resolutely at the flickering sari shop. Then at the moon. Sari shop. Moon. What messages was PP sending through the moon? She'd said she would. The moon looked back, as bland and boring as Swara felt. V. Boring! V. Unexciting! The moon looked like it was yawning. She was too.

Once again, later that night, Appa had to carry her over to the bed, knocking off her slippers and tucking her in with the orange knitted doll that his daughter had discovered love for at the late age of almost nine.

☆ ☆ ☆

Nina Miss started her online class in geography with a strange and non-geographical statement. "Today, I will not teach class," she began. In the excited chatter that erupted, she cleared her throat. "That is, you will talk. And I will learn."

The students sat in front of their computer screens in their houses, some sprawled across beds, some propped up on sofas, some made to sit on straight-backed dining chairs. All just squares on the screen.

Nina Miss started her non-class by asking, "What are you afraid of?"

"Lizards," said someone, from a little square on the screen.

"No," Nina Miss said. "Let me explain."

A trap! She'd started by saying "no class," which surely meant by her own rules that she should not have been explaining anything.

"This lockdown has put geographical boundaries around us, which are the walls of our houses. Being shut off from friends is even more distressing in this time of uncertainty. We are all afraid of what is happening, what will happen. And we have no one to talk to. So let's talk about it here. Start."

No one started, so Nina Miss said, "Okay, I will start. I am afraid that there is more incorrect information spreading than the actual virus."

The voices began slowly, and then faster and all together.

"I'm afraid this is the end of the world."

"That my hair will grow longer than my sister's."

"You can't look any funnier, don't worry."

"Shh," Nina Miss interrupted. "Stick to what you are afraid of only."

"Of my uncle."

"Why?" Nina Miss sounded alarmed. "Did he do anything?"

"No, he snores so loudly, it's like thunder."

"I'm afraid that I will get sick."

"Yes, me too."

"Me too. From the vegetables I eat. They come from the shop, and what if they have the virus?"

"I'm afraid of my dad losing his job."

"Of my mom losing her job."

"My mom is afraid of the bathroom scale."

"Of us having no money."

"Me too. What if my folks can't buy the skates they promised me?"

"Of lizards. Really. More lizards now."

"Of never playing with my friends again."

"That I will fail these online classes."

"That's because you are bouncing a ball instead of attending the class. We can see you on the screen."

"That people won't have enough to eat."

"That the world won't be normal ever again."

"That I won't get to eat out in my favorite pizza place. What if it closes down? Businesses are closing down, my papa says."

"I'm afraid that my abba will die. Everyone is keeping away from sick people, but my abba has to look after them all day."

There was silence. That was Zarir.

"No one will die! You are a liar! Everyone is a liar! No one dies! I hate you all!" And that was Swara. Screaming. Suddenly.

Nina Miss asked gently, "Swara, what are you afraid of? Is anyone sick in your family? Did something happen?"

"No. She did not die. She will come back soon. You'll see. She's sending me clues to find her again."

"Who? Swara, what are you really afraid of?"

Swara heard a voice. It was hers. "I'm afraid the world WILL go back to normal. And we will forget the people who are gone."

Tick-tock.

Tick-tock.

Tick-tock.

More silence. Nina Miss began to note down something.

Then a voice popped up again.

"I'm afraid of lizards. Nina Miss, please write that down too."

"I'm afraid I will have to eat my mom's cooking forever."

Everyone in every box on the screen began to laugh. But not Swara.

And Nina Miss kept writing. It was about Swara—she knew it was. Nina Miss would call Amma-Appa. And give them more stress. And give Amma more reasons to Not Really Cry.

On top of everything else, she decided she was now afraid of online classes.

# Ghosts in Saris

Lowered voices. Grown-ups should know by now that that's a sign for kids to listen in even more. Ears to door, floor, wherever. If kids could detach their ears and send them places to eavesdrop, they would.

Swara leaned against their bedroom door. She'd come in toward the tail end (just a saying) of the conversation. The blanks are where she couldn't hear the whole bit.

"All I'm saying is, 'what if?'" Appa's voice was cajoling.

"No, it won't happen." From Amma.

"It's happening. All over. Suresh phoned me last

week, _____ has put him on a month's notice. _____ too. And he's been there for half his working life."

"That's not fair. They should not do this to _____ people." Amma sounded like she was about to cry/ was crying/had cried.

"Got nothing to do with fair. It's about _____." Swara could guess this one because she'd learned it at school: All is fair in love and war. *Which one was this?* she wondered.

"I don't care about economics!" Amma shouted. That didn't make sense with "in love and war." Also, it was Rishi who was studying economics. Swara tucked her unruly curls away from her ear to press it closer to the door.

"All I'm saying is I, too, could be. We need to be prepared, that's all." Appa was using that voice, which actually meant "please, help me."

"But we can't leave."

What? Swara stood back. Leave? Amma too? Where? Why?

Appa launched into a long speech that was full of

blanks because Swara's mind was still reeling with the leaving bit. "If _____, then we can't _____ this rent. And until I find a new job, which is tough in _____, we need a place to live. So if I get _____, we should relocate to_____."

"No," Amma said. "I can't leave. You go if you must. I will stay here with the kids."

"How can we do that? _____ for a short while till I find _____."

"No."

"Please. At least we have a home in Madurai, where my parents live."

Hunnnnhhhhh. Swara must have said that aloud, because there was a sudden shush. She rushed into the bathroom and turned on the faucet, splashing her face furiously, pretending she'd been there a long time.

Her father wanted them to leave Bengaluru, all their friends and school and everything.

Her mother wanted to split up their family.

Swara would never leave. Never. Never.

She would never leave, because that meant giving up on Pitter Paati and leaving her behind.

She would run away. Only, how could she, when there was a lockdown and they couldn't even put a toe outside the door?

☆ ☆ ☆

It was V. Impossible to concentrate on anything, neither on homework nor on finding clues, after hearing that. Swara had tiptoed to Rishi's room four times to tell him, but something stopped her. He was so worried about his studies. It wasn't fair to make him worry about this as well. Even if it was all fair in love and war and economics, remember?

Sitting at the window was the only thing possible. Staring at the moon made her feel better. In some way, it made sense. It was so quiet that she could replay in her mind the chats that she'd had with Pitter Paati. In a way, PP was talking to her, like she said she would.

The men on the motorbike rode in almost every night. Just after the pharmacy shutters went down and the pharmacy owner left, they'd roll in, engine and lights off, park their motorbike, and walk over to the sari shop building. She had to remind herself that there was nothing criminal happening there.

The most exciting thing about the sari shop was the mask-making rumor she'd sparked off. Or Zarir had.

She thought about Zarir.

If she was frightened about all this, he must feel so much worse. Because of his doctor father. And she had elevated it to sky-high levels by calling him a fool doctor. She'd call him, like Amma had told her earlier, to change her mistake into something brave.

"How is your father, Zarir?"

"Again? Swara, don't start again."

"No, no, I'm sorry that I called him a fool. He is brilliant and helpful. I am sorry he is looking after sick people too."

"Why?"

"Because, you know, he could also—I mean . . ."

"Someone has to look after sick people, right?" Zarir was so kind. Swara instantly felt even guiltier about her earlier intention to thrash him.

"How is your sari shop crime going?" he asked.

"Nothing. I mean, there's no crime. These two men come in every night, park far away, walk over to the building, unlock the door, go up the stairs with small backpacks on, and shine flashlights around on the third floor. And then they come down early in the morning before the sun's even risen—I once set the alarm to check. And they go off with the same small backpacks on. It's not like they're even stealing heaps of saris."

"Oh, maybe they just go there to sleep, then?" Zarir said, adding softly, "Maybe they have no homes."

Like me, Swara almost said. She almost told him about going off to Madurai soon, forever, or whatever. She almost told him she was planning to run away. She almost said all that, but she didn't.

Instead, she mentioned what had been niggling at her mind. "It's just that they look suspicious, Zarir. They ride in with their motorbike lights and engine off, then they kind of creep toward the building."

"Let it go, Swara. Bye. Talk tomorrow."

Instead, Swara called him back in five minutes, hysterical. "I got it, Zarir! If they go there to sleep, why are they flashing lights all night? No one sleeps like that."

Obviously, Swara wouldn't let it go. That was the kind of detective that Pitter Paati liked. Little Miss Marble would follow that sari trail till its very end.

☆ ☆ ☆

If you really truly believe in something, it will happen. Swara read that somewhere, and it had happened.

All the nonbelievers in the world (or at least in her family, Anand Maama topping the current blacklist) would now regret their disbelief.

Swara had found a clue.

Supernaturally received because she, for sure, hadn't put it there. A clue. Two clues. Well, one, because they were connected.

She'd woken early to catch the sari shop criminals leaving, and then felt miserable. Even more useless than usual. Completely unable to control the circumstances that were spinning her world around. Drowning in the anxiety that filled the house, emanating from the TV, pouring out of phone calls.

She went to play with her long-ignored action heroes. They had superpowers. They would make her feel like she could save the world. Digging into the shoebox where they lay, she picked up Spidey—and he had boots on!

Not his usual ones, but yellow knitted ones.

Booties. The kind that babies wear. With yellow ribbons tied into bows. Spidey wouldn't really be seen dead with ribbons on his boots. Especially boots that were way too big for him. But there he was.

The shock of it knocked her backward (saying, saying!).

She'd almost stopped believing that Pitter Paati would communicate, and there she was, snorting at her grandkid's ignorance. Humph, humph, like she used to go if anyone questioned the existence of things like ghosts or magic.

Swara pulled the booties off Spidey and charged into where Amma sat, awake even at that early hour, typing on her laptop. She shook her mother's shoulder. "Look!" she said. "It's a clue. No one believed me, but Pitter Paati is sending me messages. Out of nowhere, Spidey had these on, look! He went into his box without them, and days later, he's emerged with them on."

Amma was looking at her almost-nine-year-old strangely while Swara waved the booties in front of her face.

"Why are you staring like that, Amma? Aren't

these clues? Oh, these aren't Pitter Paati's booties. These are too small. These are baby booties." Swara felt deflated. "It doesn't make sense. Nothing makes sense."

"It does make sense," Amma said, surprisingly. Surprising because Swara's mother was usually such a practical one, wasn't she? "Your grandmother didn't wear these booties. But she knitted them. For me, when I was a baby. Then Anand Maama wore them. Then Rishi. And then you."

Swara stared at the yellow booties while Amma continued with the hint of a smile. "Perhaps she means these booties to be for your babies now?"

"Yeah!" Swara shouted in triumph, fist-pumping the air. "Like for Spidey."

Amma smiled and said, "The love goes on and on . . ."

The world was back on its axis. The sun was shining once again. The clue was a clue. Swara said in wonder, "She sent me a clue. I wish I was as smart as Pitter Paati."

"You are, Swara."

"No. I can't even find her. I can't even do that. I

can't follow clues. I bet if she had to look for me, she'd find me real fast."

Amma said nothing, so Swara continued, the see-saw of emotions taking her back under, making her feel V. Stupid and V. Sorry for herself again. "I can't do half the things Pitter Paati could."

"You could try. You could try knitting. Would you like to learn to knit like Pitter Paati?"

And that's how they spent the next couple of days. Amma and Swara. They pulled out PP's knitting needles and wool. Amma was clueless, unfortunately, about knitting, so they looked up online videos, and the knitting marathon began.

It wasn't tough. Needle in. Loop the wool around. Needle twist. Pull the loop off.

Swara knitted nonstop.

Swara knitted and knitted.

Every spare minute of the day.

Even though her fingers grew red.

She knitted a long, long strip of yellow, then added green, then pink, then orange.

Amma said, "Your hands look just like Pitter Paati's while you're knitting. Magical! So beautiful, Swara. So gifted."

Swara knitted even more passionately after that. While sitting in online classes. While looking out of the window at the sari shop. While watching TV.

Rishi asked in passing, "What are you doing, Boondi?"

"What's it look like?"

"Nothing, that's why I'm asking. It's a long strip. Oh, I know—it's a skipping rope!"

"Go away!"

"Okay, then, a puppy leash for the puppy that you'll never get."

"Go away! I didn't ask you."

"Ah yes! It's to pull out the poisonous papaya from inside your stomach . . ."

"Ammaaaaaaaa! Rishi is bothering me!"

She knitted while leaning against the door, listening to Amma-Appa whispering. While waiting for the moon to send messages. While everyone thought she was studying. While everyone thought she was sleeping. While sitting and chatting with Ruth in the doorway.

"Ruth, I know what's happening in that sari shop!"

"What is it? Not that I care!" Ruth had been sulking because her mom had scolded her too about the mask-making rumor that spread in their building group.

"Ghosts!"

"There are no ghosts. You're just a baby!"

"I'm not. I'm almost nine. Explain this, then. The lights? Those flashing lights. They go through walls. And humans can't go through walls."

Ruth leaned in, wide-eyed. "Like? Tell me more."

"Those men, they go into the sari shop and turn into ghosts every night."

"Why? How?"

"So, I've been knitting at the window, yeah? I saw lights in the sari shop. Then I saw them in the shop below, which is the . . ."

"Salon," said Ruth.

"There, yes. All those are locked-up shops. No one goes in and out. No one can. But the dancing lights go

through. Salon, sari shop. Now they're going over to the next building that's hugging that one. The second floor where that place sells lamps. There too."

"They dance around, these ghosts? I mean lights? They dance?"

"Yes."

"What kind of dance?" Ruth swayed, arms out.

"Not that kind of dance. Like on and off. Dim and bright."

"Maybe they are hypnotizing you. Don't look, Swara."

"Sometimes they flash up in the sari shop, sometimes in the salon below, sometimes in the lamp shop next to it, sometimes back in the salon. Sometimes in both the sari shop and the lamp shop at the same time."

Ruth leaned out over the landing, forgetting her own rules. "Can I come look too? My apartment faces the other side, so I can't see the street. I can sneak in late at night if you open your door for me."

"No!" Swara said, extremely righteous. "Your toes will get purple and fall off, remember?"

# A Stunning Discovery

The most V. Unbelievable, V. Exciting thing happened during the lockdown. The answer to a little girl's heart's deepest wish. Well, to be fair, the wish wasn't buried so deep that no one knew about it. In fact, everyone did.

Swara had wailed, on and off, through the years, "I want a puppy!"

"I want a puppy puppy puppy puppy puppy puppy puppy puppy puppy." Swara stopped for a breath. "I wanta puppy puppy puppy puppy puppy puppy puppy." Rishi covered her mouth.

"M pppp u u u pppppp e e e e mffffupppppeeeeee." Swara bit Rishi's fingers. "Ammaaaaa, look at Rishi! I want a puppy puppy puppy puppy puppy puppy puppy

puppy puppy puppy puppy puppy puppy puppy puppy puppy puppy puppy puppy puppy puppy puppy puppy puppy . . ."

This had gone on for hours, days, years.

Amma had said every time, "Puppies aren't toys. They are lifelong commitments. You can't just play with one and then get tired of it and put it on a shelf."

"I will feed it and bathe it and walk it and love it. I want a puppy puppy puppy puppy puppy puppy puppy puppy puppy . . ."

"Remember, Swara, how you wanted that dinosaur book? Where is it now?"

Swara had no idea. But Amma did. "I found it fallen behind the bookshelf."

Appa had been stubborn as well. "We love puppies too, Swara. But they become big, and when they stop being funny and cute, would you still want one? Do you know how many abandoned puppies live in shelters or on the streets because people got fed up with taking care of them?"

"I won't be like those V. Awful, V. Horrible people. I will love my puppy forever. The only thing I want in the world is a puppy puppy puppy."

"Remember when the only thing you wanted in the world was Iron Man?" This came from Traitor Rishi.

Swara had tried every battle maneuver. "A dog is a man's best friend."

"And you're not a man!" Rishi had said. He was just being V. Annoying. Swara knew he too wanted a puppy puppy puppy.

She had waited for a puppy on her sixth birthday, but had gotten a kiddie laptop. (Educational toy—ugh!)

She had waited for a puppy on her seventh birthday, but had gotten a bicycle.

She had waited for a puppy on her eighth birthday, but had gotten a basketball set, hoop and all. (Also gathering dust on top of the bookshelf now. Oops!)

She was now almost nine, her birthday was coming up, and she'd given up on waiting for the puppy.

No one cared for a little girl's heart's deepest wish, it was V. Obvious! No one cared for her except You-Know-Who!

This backstory is only to explain how exciting it was when the most V. Unbelievable, V. Exciting thing happened.

Swara woke up in the middle of the night. She was cold, and she thought she'd woken up to—you know—do the thing that everyone mostly wakes up in the middle of the night for. Sleepwalk to the toilet. Then she heard that sound again.

She rubbed the sleep from her eyes and stared out at the moon. Then at the sari shop.

Whimpering. Scratching. Howling.

Ghosts!

No, the sound came from outside their front door. Had the dancing ghosts entered her building?

Since you obviously know by now what it is, let's cut out all the suspense.

Swara bounced out of her room, opened the locks and chains, and yanked open the door. She was over the moon (just a saying) to see a puppy tied with a ragged string to her doorpost. The puppy was equally over the moon (still a saying—it was the cow who jumped over the moon in that rhyme, not a puppy!) to see her.

"Ammaaaaaaa! Appaaaaaaaa!" Swara yelled while sinking to her knees and pulling the squirming brown-and-white puppy onto her lap.

Lights flicked on and footsteps sounded from bedrooms.

Swara was so hysterical that no words came out. She kept holding up the puppy to everyone who walked in.

Then everything came out with stutters. "You can't say no. No, no, you can't. Look, the puppy just came here. Just came home. To me. For me. Please don't say no."

Appa, smiling, unhooked the puppy from the length of dirty string. "Now, who would leave a tiny puppy all alone outside our house?"

"Pitter Paati!" Swara yelled. She launched her appeal again, louder. "It's a clue! That's what it is. You never let me have a puppy. So Pitter Paati sent this one over. You can't say no to Pitter Paati. She's older than you!" She ended on irrefutable logic.

Amma sighed. "I guess we can't say no, then."

Swara squealed in glee and danced the way Viru had, throwing her shoulders from one side to the other. The puppy jumped at her, quite oblivious of why she was celebrating but willing to join in. That's the way puppies are—you know if you've had the honor of having one.

Amma had disappeared into the kitchen, and she now emerged with a plastic bowl of water. Rishi tore open a pack of strange biscuits he took from the back of a high cupboard. Appa managed to find the oldest hairbrush she had ever seen. If you had a suspicious mind, you'd have thought that they were prepared for something so unexpected, unbelievable, exciting. If you had a suspicious mind . . . which you hopefully haven't.

Swara looked on, speechless, while the puppy was brushed, cleaned, and fed.

Slowly, something sank deep into her heart. Was it the deepest wish that sank deeper? She said softly, "I don't want a puppy."

Appa stopped and looked up at her, brush in hand. "But, Swara, you have wanted a puppy as a birthday gift every single birthday so far."

"I don't want anyone else to love" is what she said.

*Because they all just go away* is what she didn't say. Thought, but didn't say.

There were too many feelings bottled up inside Swara, jostling for space in her heart, so the deepest wish had to make room for them. She turned away and ran back to her room. Once she'd banged the door shut, she sat and looked at the moon and allowed herself, for the first time, to really cry.

☆ ☆ ☆

On the heels of the most V. Exciting day of the lockdown came the V. Rottenest.

Swara woke to see Pitter Paati smiling down at her from up on the living room wall. From a big photograph, which Swara knew had been printed on their home printer. She was in the golden frame that used to have a picture of Amma-Appa, Rishi, and herself as a baby. She certainly had looked like a boondi ladoo in that photo, she admitted to herself. Round and golden and shiny. She was a smiley baby because she didn't know how V. Rotten life would become. All she knew then was that her thumb tasted good when she sucked on it.

Seeing Pitter Paati's photograph up on the wall, her larger-than-life face, should have made Swara feel great. Being always able to look at her now. But it meant much more, didn't it? At almost nine, Swara knew what it meant. Or what her family thought it meant.

Pictures of big faces all by themselves didn't just go up when the people-of-the-faces were hopping around. They went up when you didn't expect to see the person again, which was why you put up a picture to remember them by.

As if anyone needed a picture for that. Pitter Paati was always on her mind. About thirty-three thousand times a day. Or at least thirty-three. Or even three. Only three? Was she forgetting her most favorite person in the world already?

Swara ignored the photograph and what it meant.

Swara ignored the puppy, which was tougher to ignore, jumping and falling and rolling and squeaking, chasing the shifting sunlight beams that threw patterns across the living room floor. Such a bundle of silliness! Rishi was playing with the puppy instead of staying locked in his room, studying all the time. Appa kept tickling the puppy's ears while taking the phone calls. Swara noticed Amma even breaking into a smile often as the puppy tried to tug at her pajamas.

Swara sat glumly, staring at her teacher in her online class. She could not focus at all on Hindi lessons. Or math. Or anything. Not on the mock quiz. Not on the video presentation. Not on the Q and A. Not even on the jokes that her classmates cracked.

She sat with a frown that sliced into her brow. She kept stealing a look at the puppy's latest antics when no one could see her. Let the V. Silly puppy act all excited and cute. She would not love anyone again. It was a trap!

After dinner, Swara shut her bedroom door. Anyway, the puppy had adopted Rishi's room for the nights. She was already feeling a little left out. Not even the newest little member of the family cared about her. No one cared, except You-Know-Who.

She tiptoed out into the living room when all the lights had gone off in the house, to have a word or two with You-Know-Who. In the glow of the streetlights from outside, and from the security cabin downstairs, and the occasional high beam of a passing vehicle, Swara looked at Pitter Paati.

She'd always talked to her about whatever was on her mind. "Where are you? And will you come back or not? Where are all the messages you said you'd send me?" Pitter Paati looked straight ahead, with that twinkle in her eye, which you could see even through her thick pink-framed spectacles.

Swara wouldn't let up. She was angry. "You don't care either. No one cares. And you aren't helping me solve the mystery across the street. Is there even a mystery? You're not telling me anything. What's the point of calling me your Little Miss Marble and then not helping?"

A beam from a passing headlight caught Pitter Paati's face, lighting it up. Then it went dark again. Then another light flashed on it. On. Off. On. For a few minutes.

Swara gasped. Of course. That was it!

There was a mystery. There was a crime happening. And it was Pitter Paati who, from inside her frame on the wall, had helped her. Just like she said she would. Swara went up on tiptoes and planted a kiss on the photograph.

She scuttled back to her room and sat at the window, focusing on the lights in the sari shop.

On. Off. On. On. On. On. Off.

She got it. Every time the patrol policemen on their motorcycle passed, the lights would go off. The ghost men didn't want to be seen. They were up to no good, as Thaatha would put it. "Those fools! They are up to no good!" He said this about almost everyone, of course, including teenagers and pigeons.

Swara was certain that something was happening across the street that shouldn't be happening. They were careful not to be seen by the police. She trained her eyes on the sari shop. The lights were now flashing from the lamp shop in the next building. She waited.

After fifteen minutes, she heard the faint rumble of a motorcycle and she noticed the lights across the street go off. It was some random bike tearing past. The lights flashed back on. In another ten minutes, the police motorcycle roared into view and slowly rolled by. The lights had immediately gone off, and only when the policemen had passed out of sight did the lights begin to blink again.

Swara gulped. "Thanks, Pitter Paati," she whispered.

The next morning, a bleary-eyed Swara walked into the dining room, clutching her orange knitted doll. A Saturday meant no class. She wondered how detectives managed to stay up all night, sneaking around in dark alleys, without falling asleep into their breakfast bowls the next day.

She was late, and her bowl of rice porridge was left on the table, covered with a plate. She winked at Pitter Paati up on the wall and settled herself down to the task of eating. Cold, lumpy porridge was usually reason to chew exaggeratedly with a face as thunderous as she could muster, but not during the lockdown, when no Akka came over to cook. Amma had to manage most of it, so Appa made it clear that any food was good food. He tried helping out in the kitchen, but his cooking was even worse. Rishi was the most promising chef among them all, but he had spent the lockdown with a DO NOT DISTURB poster glued to his door.

Breakfast done, she carried her empty bowl to the kitchen, where she found Amma-Appa—Amma wiping down packages and Appa putting them away. Oh, groceries bought already? This meant (to a V. Exceptional detective like Little Miss Marble) two things:

One, that they had enough money to buy groceries. They would eat! Phew! She had been really worried that they were really worried about that.

Two, that they would not be leaving home and going to Madurai that week. They were staying for a while, at least. Phew again!

From the other direction, an arm movement caught her eye. Out on the balcony, Rishi was on his knees, bent over a potted plant. Rishi gardening? Humph! The puppy was also digging in the mud, squealing with glee.

Swara had to investigate. She strolled out. "What are you doing?"

Rishi kept his head lowered and kept digging a hole in the mud in the pot. Beside him lay clippers, a trowel, gloves, a watering can, and a plant with its roots tied up in a packet. He was scowling. The puppy wasn't as surly and seemed delighted to see her.

"What are you doing? Are you looking for clues too?" Swara asked louder.

"Go away, Swara! Don't poke your nose into other people's business."

That, of course, was an invitation, like any sibling knows, to poke her nose in further. Well, if the puppy could literally poke a nose into the mud, why not her?

"You NEVER do anything with the plants. Tell me what you're doing now."

"I'm burying treasure. Happy?"

Of course, that was not what he was doing. He was making fun of her, like she didn't know that. Fool Rishi!

She picked up the plant in its packet. "What's this?"

To her shock, Rishi swatted her hand. He snapped, "Get out of here! Give me that."

Swara's lip began to tremble, and Rishi stopped digging. He covered his face with his muddy hands. They stayed frozen like that for almost an entire minute. Then he said, "Boondi, this is a karuvepillai plant. Curry leaf. You know how Pitter Paati couldn't cook anything without throwing a handful of curry leaves into the oil first? I am growing them in her memor—for her. Appa got me a cutting from the market. Here. Now we can grow our own curry leaves, and we can feel like she's here, close to us, feeding us spicy food. Right?"

Swara nodded, absently stroking the puppy, who'd turned belly-up on the muddy floor.

She what? She hadn't realized what she was doing. She was melting. She was patting and tickling and loving the puppy. No! She sighed.

Rishi was all choked up. He did care about Pitter Paati. She knew it!

Swara pulled another clay pot toward her and took up the heavy yellow-handled trowel. She began to dig at the mud too.

"Now what are you doing, silly Boondi?" But he said it fondly, not angrily.

"I'm going to plant a mango tree, Rishi. You love mangoes. So when you go away to college next year, I will look at this mango tree and feel you're close by too."

Two more things that a V. Exceptional detective like Little Miss Marble found out that day:

One, that loving someone new doesn't mean you stop missing the old one.

Two, that boys do cry.

# Proof of Crime

The puppy and the girl became inseparable after that. That's what Rishi said every time they appeared. "Here comes the mighty twinned two-for-the-price-of-one perma-glued Boonpupoondi." If you've figured out that Swara couldn't take hearing that anymore, you will realize, as Swara did, that the puppy couldn't be called Puppy or this and that any longer.

She was determined that the puppy get a name linking both herself and Pitter Paati. After all, PP was the one who had sent the puppy over somehow, since no one else in Swara's family "cared," as she complained often enough.

After a day of thinking and consulting Zarir and Ruth, she announced the puppy would henceforth go by the name of Little Miss Muffet. It reminded Swara of Pitter Paati, and it fit quite snugly into the detective theme.

"The puppy is male," Rishi scoffed. "He's not Little Miss anything."

As Swara deliberated over an entire day's plotting coming to zilch, Amma came to Swara's rescue. "The puppy will be happy with any name chosen out of love. So Little Miss Muffet is quite acceptable."

Swara agreed. V. Acceptable. Little Miss Muffet it was! Even though Muffet didn't respond to Muffet at all.

"Sit, Muffet." Muffet jumped all over her.

"Jump, Muffet." Muffet ran off, barking.

"Sleep, Muffet." Muffet began to dig up the carpet.

"Stop, Muffet!" Muffet dug some more.

"Come here, Muffet!" Muffet curled up to sleep, tired of Swara's barking.

Swara appealed to Pitter Paati on the wall. "Little Miss Muffet is so disobedient. He sleeps when he's told to come and digs when he's told to . . . Wait!"

Yes, another breakthrough!

Ever since Pitter Paati climbed up on that wall,

she'd been sending major discoveries Swara's way. This demanded another kiss. Swara leaned up to plant a few more kisses on Pitter Paati's photograph.

Amma, supposedly reading her book, sent a smile their way.

Appa, on the sofa beside Amma, sent a smile Amma's way.

Swara sent a smile Muffet's way.

Muffet was asleep, as mentioned earlier, so the smile train stopped there. But he did contribute to a huge discovery in the mystery across the street. And so, Swara decided, he had already started earning his name. Now, if only he'd realize it was his name.

☆ ☆ ☆

Appa was watching back-to-back videos of something. Movie clips. Songs. Swara and Muffet climbed up on the sofa beside him to ask why. Swara had decided that she would be Muffet's human voice: "Wassup? Muffet wants to know."

Appa said his favorite actor had passed away, and he was just reliving happier moments.

"I hate the virus!" Swara proclaimed, disgusted.

"It wasn't coronavirus. It was cancer," said Appa.

"I hate that too. Why can't everyone be healthy and happy forever and ever?"

Appa had no answer to that. If you remember, only Pitter Paati had answers to these kinds of questions.

Swara was about to leave when he said, "Wait, Swara."

He swiped up on his phone. Swara looked on. Muffet, once dissuaded from chewing on the phone, ran off to greener pastures (saying, saying—no one could put a toe out into any pasture, whatever its color). Appa swiped up one story after the other. It was the news. But here's the strange thing. The news wasn't awful. Perhaps the news had moods too?

After a grueling stint at saving lives, a nurse got home to a standing ovation from every neighbor standing outside.

A war veteran, almost one hundred years old, had walked the length of his garden one hundred times to raise money for medical staff in his country. Swara asked if she could do that. But apparently, it only mattered when you were almost one hundred, not almost nine.

People were out on the streets feeding stray dogs because the hotels from which they got their scraps were closed.

The police in Delhi rode on motorcycles from hospital to hospital to salute the health care workers.

People were cooking meals for those on the streets.

"See, Swara?" Appa said. "It's never complete darkness. You can always find a shimmer of light, some hope, some kindness. From even the worst times comes some good."

Swara said, "Every cloud has a silver lining."

Appa tousled her hair.

Swara, encouraged, told him about the sari shop. "Appa, I, too, have a silver lining. Something exciting is happening. You know that sari shop across the street?"

"No, which one is the sari shop?"

"The one on the third floor."

"Ah, now I know." (He didn't. Appa knew nothing about shops.) "That sounds exciting, Swara."

"Appa, the story isn't over. The exciting bit is that there are men who go in there every night and turn into ghosts."

"Swara!"

"Really, Appa. I know you don't believe in ghosts and all. But Pitter Paati did. And she is the one who showed me the clues. OKAY, so maybe not ghosts. But they are up to no good, Appa. They are criminals. They are probably killing or kidnapping people in there."

"Have you seen them dragging people in there? Or are the victims ghosts too?" He was trying to hide his smile.

"No. No, just those two men. No one else goes in."

"So, you find this sari shop exciting because . . . ?"

"Because there are dancing lights."

"Dancing ghosts do seem quite exciting, I agree."

"Appa! Take me seriously! Please! Something scary is happening, can't you see? They dance through the walls every night."

"Ghosts who go into the sari shop to dance through the walls all night long?"

"Appa! They are doing something evil in there."

"Swara, I am usually very proud of your active imagination. But this time—"

"You have to believe me, Appa. Pitter Paati would have. She is the one who's sending me clues."

"Swara Baby, I know you miss your grandmother terribly. But you have to draw a line between what is real and what you wish could be real."

"It's not fair! You're the one who said good things come out of bad."

"And these kidnappers are good how?"

Swara stomped off. "You won't understand!" She threw that over her shoulder. So much for silver linings. Grown-ups never understood. Except for You-Know-Who. Who, Swara could have sworn, let out a sigh as she passed the frame on the wall. Who else could it have been? Muffet hadn't taken to sighing yet.

☆ ☆ ☆

Little Miss Marble planned it carefully.

The stakeout would be her job. The others on the detective squad didn't know they were on it yet. Therefore, they had to be cleverly enlisted. Muffet was just a novice, a trainee detective, so he couldn't be counted on to do much.

Zarir was the first to be called. "You must promise not to tell anyone. Not like you told them about the sari-mask thing," Swara began.

"What sari-mask thing?" (Ha, that ruled out Zarir. Ruth, for sure then, had spread the rumor. Fool Ruth!)

"Zarir, we need to collaborate on a very important mission."

"What mission?"

"Patience! It is about the crime in the sari shop."

"What crime?"

"Zarir, just listen, don't interrupt. I know what's happening in the sari shop, and only we can stop it."

"What's happening?"

"No one believes me, so if you promise on . . . on your new four-speed bike that you won't tell anyone, then I will tell you."

Zarir was so confused by then that the only option was to make the promise. In return, Swara told him her master plan. Zarir was enlisted.

Across the landing next.

Ruth had her hairbrush-mic out. "This is Ruth of the Matter to report that no one has been cutting the grass on the lawn or cleaning the drains since the lockdown began. Mosquitoes are breeding. We will now have malaria and dengue fever as well."

"This is Swara reporting from the ground. You must promise not to tell anyone. Not like you told them about the sari-mask thing."

Ruth waved her hairbrush around imperiously. "No threats will intimidate the Ruth from spreading news. It is the role of Ruth of the Matter to report the Ruth, the whole Ruth, and nothing—"

"But it wasn't the Ruth. The truth. The sari-mask thing was a secret. And I have another one that I won't tell you if you blabber it all around."

"Over millions of years, millions of people have been killed for telling the Ruth."

"Ruth, do you want to be part of this dangerous mission or not? Zarir is in!"

That was a bit too much for Ruth. "Okay, okay. No mic, see? This is off the record. And how dare you tell Zarir before me?"

"Ruth, we need to stop the crime in the sari shop."

"How? When we cannot even put a toe out of our homes?"

"We can. We can go out for essential things."

"What's essential? Buying a sari?"

"Patience, Ruth!" Swara was fed up with her friends. Was she the only one who was swimming in patience, almost drowning in it every night till she fell asleep?

Anyway, after a dozen interruptions and questions, she finally got the briefing of the mission across to Ruth, who promised not to open her mouth about it.

That was subdetective #2 on the squad. Now on to the most important member of them all . . .

"Rishi, I need your help."

"I'm studying. Go play with Dog-man."

"Who?"

"Trumpet. Frumpet. Your Little Miss Lumpet."

"His name is Muffet. Rishi, listen. I have a V. Dangerous V. Secret master plan, which you have to promise to help out in and not tell anyone about."

"No. Your offer is rejected!"

"Rishi, you can help stop a crime. Doesn't that inspire you?"

"No."

"Pitter Paati would have been proud."

"No, she wouldn't. Go away and play with Bucket."

"Okay. Then I will tell Amma-Appa that you *l-o-v-e* Debbie."

Rishi was enlisted! That was #3 and the main investigator.

☆ ☆ ☆

The moon was out that night, spilling its silver across the empty streets. A perfect night.

For what? Patience!

What Swara observed is true. No one has patience anymore.

"Thank you, Pitter Paati," Swara said to the photograph, "for sending me moonlight."

Moonlight for what? Surely you're wishing Ruth had leaked the secret this time. Patience, patience!

Swara kicked her plan into action after dinner. As she sat at her window knitting, she spotted the motorbike drawing up. The men, as usual, looked around furtively, scurried over to the building three doors away, and quickly went in.

Rishi was leaning over her shoulder by then, also looking through the window.

"Okay, Boondi, I am doing this for you. If only to

prove to you what a silly little Miss Muffet you are."
He planted a kiss on the top of her head.

"I'm Miss Marble, he's Miss Muffet," Swara wailed
to the disappearing back of her brother.

Rishi said to Amma-Appa, who were on the sofa
watching the news, "I have run out of my eye drops."
Rishi pinched at his eyes, wincing. "My eyes are on
fire. I'm popping out to the pharmacy to get a bottle."

Amma-Appa's voices rose anxiously at once. Since
parents get around to saying the same things, here is
what they said, and you can figure out who said what.

"Are you sure there isn't a spare bottle? I always tell
you, Rishi, to stock up on spares."

"It's too late. Can't you wait till morning?"

"The pharmacy will be closed."

"It's not safe."

"Can't we ask in the building group? Someone will
have eye drops."

"I need these prescription eye drops that Zarir's
dad recommended," Rishi said.

After convincing his parents that he couldn't study
because his eyes were burning, and he had no time to
waste arguing while the pharmacy could be shutting

down that moment, and he'd double it up with Muffet's walk, and yes, yes, he had a mask, Rishi left.

Swara hung out of her window and saw Rishi stop at the security cabin first and exchange a word with an overly concerned Govind Uncle.

Swara watched them dash across the street.

The pharmacy was shut, of course. Rishi knew that. Swara knew that. The two men only ever appeared after the pharmacy had drawn its shutters down.

Muffet sniffed at the motorbike. Good dog, Muffet! He was already on the trail. To her dismay, he then lifted a leg at it.

Rishi pulled him away and walked over casually to the building with the sari shop. Swara could see the sporadic lights on already. The lights were also flashing in the salon below by then. Rishi held his phone up.

"Has he got it?"

Swara jumped out of her skin (saying, saying). Appa had come up behind Swara.

"What? Got what?" Swara's voice trembled. Did Appa know what Rishi was trying to get?

"The eye drops."

"No." Swara gulped. "The pharmacy is closed."

"I told him that. I'll ask Dr. Ansari if he has spare drops. What's he doing now? Why isn't he coming home?"

Swara needed an immediate distraction. She couldn't think of one. But Pitter Paati, of course, came to her rescue. Her knitting! The knitting that Swara had in her hands. She dangled her arm out of the window and let one of the knitting needles drop. It was a huge sacrifice. What if PP's precious knitting needle broke or bent? Swara sent up a wail. "I want it back. Go get it back. Go, Appa, please. Please please please please." Extra pleases always worked.

"Really, Swara!" Appa hurried off, muttering.

After a few minutes, she saw him emerge one story down, looking for the knitting needle in the hedge below her window. Rishi, too, had returned by then and stumbled across Appa scrambling around in the hedge. Muffet, she was proud to say, found an old tennis ball and someone's sock. Appa found the knitting needle.

Back home, Rishi whispered to Swara, "You may

be right, Boondi. I heard it. Loud. I recorded it on my phone too. And managed to take a video of the lights."

Swara pumped her fist in the air. Then, to Rishi's surprise, she blew a kiss to the moon.

So what if she couldn't see Pitter Paati? Her grandmother was part of everything she did.

# One Mystery Solved, at Least

Something suspicious was afoot!

The last two mornings, Amma had been disappearing. Fox leather bag. Mask. And off she went.

On Day 1, Swara was indignant. Didn't Amma realize that she was not allowed to go out? It was a LOCKDOWN.

On Day 2, Swara was furious. Amma wanted to go and get sick too? And then get lost Don't Know Where like You-Know-Who?

A stray thought lodged in Swara's mind. Was Amma sneaking out to see Pitter Paati? Had she been correct all along in assuming PP was in hiding somewhere?

Of course. That was it! Elementary, my dear Watson, as PP used to say. Because, let's face facts, Amma wouldn't go out for any other reason—she couldn't. She would get arrested or infected or some other -ed.

On Day 3, Swara stood at the door, arms crossed, like a police inspector—detective police inspector, to be exact. Not the traffic one. Because he wouldn't be very effective then, standing with his arms crossed while cars crisscrossed each other.

"I know where you're going," she said.

Since Amma didn't reply, she carried on. "You're going to see Pitter Paati. And you're not telling me because you don't want to take me along."

To her surprise, Amma sat down again, her face crumpling up. Oh no!

"No, my little kitty-kutty, I am not going to see your grandmother. I wish I could. But I can't, and I wish you would accept that. Look, I am going to help others like her. Grandmothers and grandfathers who cannot go out to buy their own groceries. I am part of a group that buys them things they need. They send us the shopping lists." She waved three long strips of paper.

"But why? It's V. Risky! You will get the virus from going out, Amma."

"Because, Swara, these people have no one to help them now. Their own kids are locked down in far-away lands. If Pitter Paati were alone, locked in her house, wouldn't you want someone to go help her like this?"

It was a trick question. Saying yes meant Swara was okay with Amma going out. And it was not okay. She would get sick too. And leave her. Everyone would do that. One by one.

"It is also good for me. It makes me feel better. It makes me heal, do you understand? By doing this small thing for other mothers like mine."

Swara twisted up her mouth and stomped away from Amma and her trick questions. She kept track, however. Amma was gone for two hours.

Two hours and thirteen minutes.

Plenty of time for a million viruses to infect her. The trick question had begun to seep in, however.

It had become a trick situation. The longer she sat feeling sorry for herself, the less sorry she felt.

An idea began to creep into Swara's curly-haired head. And if you have curly hair, you know something about it—the ideas stay, they never get out (like chewing gum, if you've ever had that problem).

Swara called Ruth to tell her the idea. They giggled and thought and plotted and fought.

But finally, they came up with a list . . .

Swara pulled out her school drawing book and cut some pages into four. She scribbled each of the following lines on different bits of paper, and she drew—wait, look down and you can guess what she drew.

Together, we will BEET the virus!

You are pRICEless.

We miss you BERRY much.

I YAM so proud of you.

Stay well. Stay at home. PEAS, pretty PEAS! (This was one of Ruth's ideas and one of the reasons they fought, because it was not so clever, Swara declared.)

Whatever you want, LETTUCE get it for you.

Have an EGGcellent day!

ORANGE you so excited for some fruit?

KIWI be friends?

I love you from my head TO-MA-TOES.

Till we MEAT again! (Hope this won't go to a vegetarian!)

You should have seen Amma's face the next morning when Swara gave her the notes to attach to her bags.

But since you can't, this is what Swara told Zarir later: "Let me JUICE say this. Her face became RADISH, and she said GOURD was good when He gave me to her."

☆ ☆ ☆

Swara was knitting what she proclaimed to one and all would be a scarf for Pitter Paati. She often wore scarves around her neck (to protect her throat from the cold, she said), around her face (to protect her ears from the cold, she said), and around her head, only when Swara was around (to look like Aladdin in a turban, she said).

The afternoon's quiet was suddenly shattered by Appa's shouts.

They came from the balcony, and Amma, Rishi, and Swara ran out immediately. Muffet ran in. And disappeared under Swara's bed. Oh no!

Appa held up a slipper that was now in two pieces, and the pieces themselves had rather artistically jagged edges.

"Where is that dog?" Appa fumed.

"His name is Little Miss Muffet." Swara was tired of reminding everyone that Muffet had a proper name.

"Look what he did to my slipper!" Appa pointed it at Swara.

"Shh." Amma hushed him. "You can just wear another pair. And don't leave your slippers lying around."

"That's okay for you to say. It's not your slipper." Appa stormed on. "He attacks all my things. He chewed up the leg of my chair, and it almost broke when I sat on it. Then my pair of sandals. Then my phone. Now my slipper."

"He's just a pup." Amma shrugged it off.

"He's Little Miss Muffet!" Swara shouted too. She was V. Upset with anyone targeting Muffet.

"Anyway, don't make a mountain out of a mole-hill." Amma was getting shouty as well.

"Who got this dog in the first place?" Appa was intent on making that mountain.

"You!" The next shout that wafted up in response was from downstairs. From the security cabin, Govind Uncle shouted, "You!"

They leaned over the balcony to look down at Govind Uncle, who was quite adamant that no one should start blaming him. He said, "You told me to bring up the next lost puppy I find for Swara Baby. This one was wandering around, with no mother in sight."

In the silence that followed, Rishi began to giggle. Amma joined in. After a while, even Appa couldn't help it and gave in to guffaws. It had been so long since their family had laughed. Swara tentatively joined in. This meant that Muffet was off the hook. She had to train him, though, not to attack only Appa's things. He couldn't be partial.

While they all collapsed on the balcony chairs laughing, Swara felt a twinge of guilt.

Was it okay to be laughing? Pitter Paati was gone. Had everyone bounced back so soon?

Another sad thought struck her. If Appa had arranged for the pup and Govind Uncle had brought it home, then it hadn't been Pitter Paati's gift, as she'd believed all the while.

Amma leaned over and pulled Swara close.

Mothers are mind readers, as you've probably figured out somewhere along the way. "Swara, if you believe in something, that's your reality. No one can take that away from you." She giggled. "And who do you think put that idea in Appa's head? Wasn't me, for sure."

# Turning Point

It had been a month since Pitter Paati had disappeared.

Amma lit a scented candle in front of her photograph.

Appa was busy answering people's calls.

Rishi's curry leaf plant had been growing steadily. (It would have grown even more steadily had Muffet not insisted on digging up the soil every now and then.)

Swara's scarf was ready too.

"Kitty-kutty," Amma called out. Baby names. Huh! Swara was going to turn from almost nine to nine the next week and over nine the week after. "You don't have to participate in the prayer services or calls or anything unless you really feel like it. You can remember Pitter Paati in any way that you want to. You were her special person."

Swara's chest filled up. With little rainbow-colored balloons, that's how it felt.

She remembered how torn she was when the twins were born. She was excited about becoming a big sister to her little baby cousins. She was also rather jealous that they would be living with Pitter Paati. What if PP started loving them more than she loved Swara?

She had been almost five then and had come right out with it.

Pitter Paati had assured her that her heart was elastic. It could increase to fit in more love for any more grandkids. The main space that Swara occupied was still intact, she'd said. Swara had felt V. Extremely Reassured. Let Kriti and Kolam squeeze into the edges of Pitter Paati's heart, as long as she was in the center.

She thought long and hard about what she'd like to do, and then out of the blue, it came to her. Without a message from the moon, even. Just like that. Swara went and whispered into Amma's ear in case anyone else heard and thought she was being silly.

☆ ☆ ☆

Amma helped out quite a bit in the "look." Credit ought to be given to her.

They sat in Amma-Appa's bedroom with the door shut. Not even Muffet was allowed in, though he kept scratching at the locked door, whining at the unfairness of it all. Amma opened her cupboard and pulled down a stack of her expensive saris, which were always wrapped in muslin and smelled of mothballs. She'd only wear one of these for someone's wedding. And obviously, they weren't going out for weddings or anything right then. Most happenings were being postponed. Swara knew that her cousin had postponed getting married till the lockdown lifted. Another cousin, however, couldn't postpone having her baby. Anyway, Amma still took out the expensive wedding-only saris. Swara squealed with glee.

She chose the heavily embroidered maroon sari first. It didn't feel right. She then picked out the purple one with large peacocks all over. No! Finally, Swara held up the parrot-green sari with gold embroidery on it. She cocked an eyebrow at Amma, who nodded. "Yes, this looks like the kind of sari Pitter Paati wore."

Amma helped drape the sari around Swara. She ended up looking quite paunchy because much of the sari had to be pushed into the band of her shorts. That added to the "look." Amma folded and settled Swara's T-shirt so that it looked a wee bit more like a sari blouse.

Next, they attacked the hair. Swara's hair was a jumble of curls, like PP's, so that helped. PP had always oiled her own hair into submission. So Swara sat, ready to suffer her mother's oil massage. Soon enough, however, she began to enjoy it. Mother and daughter spent fifteen minutes like that, Amma stroking her hair, drawing her fingertips across Swara's scalp, massaging it in tiny circles—long after the oil had seeped in. She then pulled the hair into a tight knot. Swara's hair was too short (and too disobedient by far) to sit in that knot, so it kept flying out. But they were getting there.

"I need a bindi!" Swara jumped up and down. Tough to accomplish that in the sari.

Once again, Amma let Swara choose. She picked

out a large red dot, which ended up covering much of her forehead. Rishi later said she looked like she'd been shot. Why is it that brothers can never be nice?

Swara stared at the mirror. Almost there, but not quite. What was missing?

Ah, Swara dashed to the chair in her room, over which she'd slung the scarf she'd been knitting. She almost fell flat on her face, because you have to learn how to be graceful in a sari. Boisterous little girls tend to trip over pleats and folds. Amma helped wrap the scarf around Swara's face. Swara looked at herself in the mirror again, her face wrapped just like Pitter Paati's used to be.

Amma excused herself and left the room. Swara struck a few PP-like poses. V. Alike! Amma returned with a pair of Rishi's spectacles. They didn't have pink frames like Pitter Paati's. In fact, they were rimless and rectangular. Fool Rishi! Nevertheless, the "look" needed spectacles. Amma promised Swara that they would fetch PP's own spectacles once the lockdown lifted.

Swara felt sad. But she also felt happy. Whoever made up these words didn't create one for both feelings together. *Shappy.* "I feel shappy, Amma," Swara said, and Amma, once again, understood.

Swara looked at herself in the mirror. Though Rishi's spectacles blurred it up, she saw Pitter Paati emerge from that reflection. She smiled a Pitter Paati smile, and the mirror smiled back. She threw out her arms toward Pitter Paati, who opened her arms back toward her.

"Wait, Swara, something's missing." Amma suddenly rose and went back to her cupboard. This time, she used a key to open the safe inside.

"Your Pitter Paati loved to look bright and shiny and dressed up. She wouldn't be seen around without her . . ." And Amma garlanded Swara with a thick, heavy gold chain. The round pendant fell almost to her waist. Maybe Swara would grow taller when she was past almost nine.

"Yes," Swara agreed. "Just like Pitter Paati's heart of gold."

That's when everything fell into place.

Not just the "look." Not a girl celebrating her beloved grandmother. Not the pendant falling into place. Not even the selfie. Because, as you know, there's no point nowadays in dressing up if you don't take a selfie to show it off.

No, what fell into place was the mystery from across the street.

It fell into place as Swara stared at herself in the mirror.

It fell into place because her grandmother with her heart of gold had sent Swara yet another sign.

☆ ☆ ☆

Swara turned around to run off, then felt the room spin. She took off Rishi's V. Silly spectacles and handed them back to Amma. Then she ran to her bedroom window, the sari pulled up and bunched in her fists. If Amma was surprised to see this strange reaction, she didn't show it. She was used to her daughter's wild whims.

Swara looked out across the street at the string of shops.

Yes, there could be no mistake now. She knew exactly what was happening out there. She knew it as surely as if Pitter Paati had sent her a direct message. Which, Swara believed, of course, was what she'd done.

This time, she would not go wrong. This time, they would plan it out properly. They would stop the crime. Because crime it was. And a really big one too.

Little Miss Marble to the rescue!

Swara beat the drum. Yelled from the rooftops. (Sayings, sayings.) She made sure she spoke at length to the detective squad: Zarir, Ruth, and its reluctant recruit, Rishi. They slipped it out over calls to the others in the towers. To the other kids, tweens, teens. Grown-ups don't always play along. And this was V. Dangerous for grown-ups to be involved in, as you will see.

# Tick-Tock

**N**ina Miss started the online class.

"The earth has lost so much of its forest cover, so much of its mineral wealth, so many species, which it had been nurturing for centuries . . . Loss happens. It's an undeniable part of life. The earth goes on. Swara has something for us about her own loss. Swara, would you like to read your poem out aloud?"

Swara was prepped already. Nina Miss had called her earlier to say she'd found out about Pitter Paati and had let the rest of her class know too. It had made Swara angry at first, and she'd protested and said wild, ugly things to Nina Miss. Then she called her teacher back and said, "Thank you," like she'd heard Appa say when he was showing exceptional manners on all those calls. Nina Miss asked Swara whether she'd like to take up some of the class time to talk about it. Or not.

Swara held up her two sheets of paper (torn out from Rishi's notebook). There were so many scratched-out lines and so much overwriting (and smudges from, you know—when she was Not Really Crying) that she had to pause many times. But no one in the little boxes on the screen interrupted. They weren't so bad after all.

Swara cleared her throat and started in a tremulous voice.

*You had to go. I know.*
*I'm almost nine, so I know why.*
  *I only wish I'd said bye-bye.*
*You didn't go fully, though.*
*You left your cushions behind.*
  *I'll make sure they're mine.*
*I'll take your spectacles too. And when I'm*
  *almost ten,*

*I'll read your Miss Marple books myself.*

*I'll keep them on my closest shelf.*

*I won't take them all.*

*Or Kriti and Kolam will cry, because they're small.*

*You left your smile behind. That's mine.*

*(Amma helped me write this line.)*

*Rishi has your curry leaves. Till he leaves.*

*I've got your brains. That's better, no?*

*You left your jokes and funny faces in my mind.*

*You left our secrets and your knitting behind.*

*I'm still sad. I'll always be.*

*I love you times infinityyyyyyy.*

*But you left all your bits and pieces for me.*

*You forgetful Pitter Paati.*

*You don't mind that I can't rhyme.*

The poem ended suddenly. And Swara did too.

Everyone in the little on-screen boxes clapped. Swara could see them through her teary eyes. She had gotten all choked up in between, and so she couldn't even say thanks.

Nina Miss continued, "Would anyone like to help Swara end the poem? Or share anything at all if you want to, about how you carry on if you lose something?"

Tick-tock.

Tick-tock.

"Swara, I can send you Sheru, my dog, for a little while. He helps me feel better."

"You can take my baby brother. For as long as you want."

"Oh yes." Swara brightened up and turned the laptop so that her class could see Muffet curled up next to her. "I've got my own puppy now. My Pitter . . . er . . . My father got him for me."

The class dissolved into everyone leaning forward in their boxes, as if they could get closer to Muffet. There was a cacophony of squeals and awws, and all those nonsense sounds that mean "cute."

Tick-tock.

"I lost my allowance. I get no pocket money now."

"Abba lost his assistant. Dr. Navneeta. She's sick too, so a new assistant comes in now."

"We lost Manju Amma. She is also in lockdown. So now Mummy-Papa have to do the housework till Manju Amma comes back to work."

"I lost my kitten. She ran off, and we can't go out now to search for her. I'm very sad."

"I lost my retainer. I'm very happy."

"You must have lost it on purpose."

"Ha, ha."

"I've not yet lost anything, but I'm worried I might. I get headaches. I worry, and I can't tell anyone because they worry more."

"Me too. Stomachaches. Very bad."

"Me too. I worry because children are carriers. What if I infect my mom and dad?"

"My mom lost her job."

"My papa's salary was cut in half."

"My papa shut down his business."

"My family had to fire their workers."

"What horrible people you are!"

Nina Miss cut in, "No judgment, please. Tell us how you're coping now instead."

Tick-tock.

"We all help. I wash the dishes after lunch."

"I wash my own clothes, so I'm better than you. Who can't wash dishes, ha!"

"We have a washing machine. So we don't have to."

"I help my mom collect money for people out of jobs."

"We play board games together, and sometimes they all let me win."

"I learned yoga."

"I keep quiet when Mom and Dad make office calls. I didn't yell even when I stubbed my toe."

"I learned to cook rice. I would have never learned otherwise."

"I pray with my grandmother every day for everyone who got sick."

"I draw pictures."

"I shoot pictures. From my window. We see so many birds now."

"You shoot birds? Poor things. You should be arrested."

"You shut up, idiot. I am kinder than you."

Nina Miss interrupted. "No judgment. No comparison, remember. Look at the many things that you've started doing. These skills will stay with you for life."

Swara said, "I learned to knit. I learned to bathe puppies. I learned to grow curry leaves. I learned to solve crimes. I learned to drape a sari. I learned to make my mother less sad."

No one made fun of Swara for bragging so much. Not bad at all.

*They really have learned what will make them stronger, better human beings,* thought Nina Miss. She was proud of them.

And just like that, the online geography class was over, once again with no lesson being taught. Or was there?

☆ ☆ ☆

Since Swara had no Topshe (Feluda's assistant) or Elementary Dear Watson (Sherlock's assistant) to record her adventures, she had to do it herself. She wrote down clues faithfully in her diary.

The detective squad was put into action doing all-night watches. Each one was given a two-hour slot. They had to call the next kid on the roster after that.

All the detective had to do was stare at the shops and report any untoward incident.

"What is an untoward incident?" Ruth muttered, understandably grumpy about her apartment not overlooking the street or the shops, and so not being part of the night watch. "You mean they have to look 'toward' the shop. If they look in the opposite direction, 'untoward,' then no one will spot anything."

"You should read more," Swara told her. "Fool!"

"You should—you should . . ." Ruth struggled with words, as you often do when seeking an appropriately biting response, but just then Muffet ran out Swara's open door right into Ruth's apartment. Ruth was thrilled about that. She banged her door shut and spent the next hour playing with Muffet in her own home, ignoring Swara's calls to return her puppy AT ONCE. It served stupid untoward Swara right.

"It's not my fault that your fool apartment doesn't look in the right direction," Swara yelled when she finally had Muffet in her arms again.

"Yes, it's very untoward," huffed Ruth as she slammed her door.

The night watch continued all week. Though no one could claim that it continued smoothly.

Rishi was always on the first watch because he was the only one old enough to stay awake past bedtime. Parents all over insist on kids sleeping at the time that parents worldwide have unanimously agreed on.

The first night, Rishi stayed up till twelve, then phoned Zarir, who stayed up from twelve to two. Zarir, in turn, phoned Viru at two. Viru slept through the ringing. And finally, his father woke up and screamed at Zarir. Viru slept through it all. Poor Zarir did not know what to do. And there was no plan B. He finally nodded off himself. And no other shifts happened that night. Swara was furious with Viru the next day and threatened to dismiss him from the detective squad.

The second night was equally bumpy. This time, Viru woke up because he didn't want to get kicked out of the squad. At four, he called Harsha. Harsha stared at the street and the shops till the streetlamps began to dance in circles. He was all of eight years old and had stayed up late with his parents watching a film, which made him doze off. He ended up hitting his head against the corner of his desk. He set up a howl, more in shock than in pain. His entire family rushed in to the rescue, and he managed to fabricate a whole lot of rubbish to keep the big secret safe. Phew!

The third night was probably the riskiest to the operation. Zarir began to call everyone at twelve fifteen. He woke up six households in his frenzy.

He finally got through to Swara and yelled hysterically that the untoward incident was happening.

Swara began to blabber excitedly, "What what what?"

"There's a truck that's stopped, and there are two men putting up a ladder."

"Aiyyo!" Swara said, just like Pitter Paati would have. She had left her bits and pieces behind, remember? "Zarir, this means they are going in. We are on top of it!"

"On top of what? The men are on top of it, the ladder, actually."

"On top of it means in control of it, Zarir. You should read more."

"But why a ladder when they could use the staircase?"

Swara had no answer to that. "Okay, bye, I'll go check now. Thank you for reporting. You have done your job. I will take over now. Wait for my next orders."

"Wait! I want to—" Zarir yelled into the dull buzz. She'd disconnected. And he was annoyed that she was grabbing the best part of it all when he had been the one to flag the untoward incident.

Swara went dashing to her window. Muffet responded to her charging around by yapping and charging around behind her. Amma-Appa and Rishi woke up and opened their doors.

Swara saw the truck parked outside the sari shop. There were men on a ladder. BUT! Fool Zarir! The men were repairing a streetlamp that had been broken for a week.

Everyone had a lot of explaining to do. To parents. To neighbors who'd been woken up. Many elaborate and improbable excuses were manufactured. These included ghosts, nightmares, lightning strikes (on a calm night), and even UFO sightings. The next day, the building group's discussion was fiery. Complaints about the wild behavior of some kids poured in. Poor

Appa! He didn't brag about Swara's exceptional manners for a good long while after that.

Swara was V. Hopping V. Mad. Her detectives were all inefficient underlings.

"Untoward underlings, you mean," Ruth said superciliously when Swara updated her the next morning. Muffet, to add insult to injury, ran into Ruth's open arms yet again. Swara complained bitterly to Pitter Paati about inefficient underlings and disloyal dogs. Fools!

☆ ☆ ☆

Rishi couldn't stop blabbering about some college he'd applied to, where the professor had taken an interest in his application and had been writing to him. All because of some stupid project he had done. Amma-Appa lapped up every word, hugging him and beaming from ear to ear.

Swara shot him the darkest looks she could muster.

She tore out some more pages of his notebook to sketch on, but even that didn't provoke him enough to scream at her.

She took Muffet into her room and refused to let him go into Rishi's room.

She even thought she'd pluck off all the leaves from Rishi's curry leaf plant and throw it into whatever was being cooked. But she stopped at that. She wasn't mean, after all, just . . . What was she feeling?

"What's up, Dumbo?" Rishi walked into her room and sat down on her bed.

Swara twisted her mouth up.

"Why are you angry with me?" Rishi found himself asking the back of her curly head.

"You're sitting on my drawing."

Rishi pulled the page out from under him and asked, "What's this?"

"Can't you see? Why do you have spectacles, then?"

"Okay, let's see, they're stick figures chasing each other. The last one has a really long hand."

"That's a stick! Not his hand."

"Okay, right. So, the first one who's running has a coconut. Got it, they are a bunch of monkeys."

Rishi did his best; you've got to give him that. He knew that Swara adored animals and was always trying to sketch them or create stories around them. She even had a series around a pig some time earlier. Good guess, in those circumstances.

Swara screamed, "It's not a coconut. It's a sack full of gold. And those are not monkeys. Those are people. The policemen with sticks are chasing the bandit with the sack."

"Oh, now that you explain it, it's just that. Why does the second man have a triangular tummy, though?"

"Because he is not a man. He . . . She is a police-woman. She is wearing a sari."

"Well drawn, Swara!" Rishi leaned over to ruffle her hair as she lay flat on her stomach on the bed. She twisted away again.

"Okay, if you won't tell me, I'll guess," Rishi started. "You're angry because my hair is better than yours."

"It's not. Mine is infinityyyyyyy times better. So is my smile, my eyes, everything—just in case you try."

"You're angry because you woke everyone up at night?"

"I did not. Zarir did. Fool!"

"You're angry because you can't draw monkeys?"

Swara threw her pencil at him. Then she held out another page to him—the one she had been sketching on.

Rishi squinted at it. He sensed this was serious. No more fooling around. This was important to her. It was probably about their beloved grandmother. And he had better get his first guess right this time. He frowned hard at the page. What did it mean?

Right at the bottom in one corner, there was a very tiny mop of jumbled wires with four sticks attached. That was probably Swara's self-portrait.

High up, in the opposite corner, was a stick figure with a triangular belly. This, he knew from recent experience, was a woman. It was Pitter Paati. She was going out through a tall rectangle. A door? Yes, that was it.

Below Pitter Paati, there was another stick figure, whose only defining characteristic was a pair of gigantic circles for eyes. Oh, that was him, Rishi, and those were his glasses. And he was leaving through a door too.

Rishi flattened himself out on the bed, next to Swara.

"Little Boondi," he said, "you think everyone is

leaving you? But I'll be back. I'm not going off anywhere for long without you. I'm kinda stuck with you, you're my sister. I can't leave you, no matter how annoying you are."

Swara's face cracked into a grin. "I am not annoying. You are. V. Annoying! Fool!"

Rishi continued, "I am fortunate to be able to go to college. And I'm going to study what I need to and, after that, come back and work here. And then I'll be able to buy you stuff you want."

"I only want one thing," Swara said.

"Yes, Boondi, but I can't bring her back. I'm sorry." Swara let Rishi put his arm around her. She burrowed her leaky nose into his T-shirt, and he didn't seem to mind.

"You, too, will go off to college someday, Swara, to what we all hope, with your brains, will be a really great one. By that time, I will be back, and I will sulk like this. I will draw pictures of coconuts and monkeys too."

This time Swara laughed.

"When will you come back?" she asked.

"I'll come back during the winter holiday to start

with. Okay? I promise you. But I have to go, you understand?"

"Okay." She nodded. "I understand. I'm almost nine."

"See?" said Rishi. "Those are the brains I was talking about. Now, if only you could draw."

She threw her pillow at him. Muffet, yapping in excitement, jumped into the rough and tumble.

Through the doorway of Swara's room, from across the hall, Pitter Paati's picture twinkled at them. Amma-Appa hid behind the curtains and smiled at each other. All because of monkeys and triangles.

# It Happened on a Tuesday

It happened on a Tuesday.

It happened on Uttara's shift, a new entrant into the detective squad, which did not please the old guard. Uttara, who was ten years old, was given the shift as a trial. The two men had not rolled up on their motorbike the night before. Therefore, the tired old detectives were given a rest, and newbies were given slots. Uttara had the midnight-to-two shift, and halfway through it, she saw something that didn't quite sit right.

A white minivan drew up across the street, the kind some kids came to school in. It rolled slowly to a halt three buildings away from the sari shop, its headlights turned off. A man got out and looked around suspiciously (according to Uttara), then crept to the door that led to the sari shop. He appeared in the sari shop window with a brick that he threw at the streetlamp outside. Uttara gasped. The streetlamp broke—again—and the light went out, sending a good portion of the street into darkness. The minivan then reversed until it was right next to the sari shop. A second man ran out and up the stairs too.

Uttara dutifully reported each detail when she called Rishi on his phone. Rishi woke Swara. They rushed to her window, and she said, "This is it! It's happening! Time to put the plan into action."

The roles were predefined and clear. Calls were made quickly.

"Agent V," whispered Swara, "go into action. Over."

Agent V replied, "Over and out." Agent V, known to the world at large as Viru, whose older brother had the best cell phone camera around, took a picture of the broken streetlamp, with the brick and shards of glass on the street below, and sent it over to Agent Z.

Zarir sent it to his father, who was putting in a night shift at the hospital. He then followed up with a call and had to use all his persuasive powers and a good five minutes that they could ill afford to convince his father about the crime going on across the street and to ask him to call the local police station. The detective squad had this planned out. If the call came from Zarir's doctor father, it would be treated seriously—more seriously than if it were coming in from a kid.

Agent R then picked up Subagent M's leash to take him down for a walk in the middle of the night. It was the only excuse Rishi could think of, had his parents woken up. Muffet, after all, was known to want to pee at the strangest hours.

"Wait!" Swara hissed.

"What?" Rishi said impatiently. "There's no time to waste now."

"Wait!" Swara ran up to him with something in her hands. It was the mask she'd painted on for Pitter Paati, and which had not been given to her. "This will keep you safe."

Rishi gave her the second hug of the week. Totally unprecedented times. Usually it was a thump or a tickle.

Swara took up watch at her window. She saw Rishi

downstairs, explaining something through frantic gestures to Govind Uncle in his security cabin.

He seemed to have done a decent job of convincing him, because they both emerged through the main gate, looking out at the street.

The rest of the detective squad (and some irritable parents) had also been awakened. As a result, there were many detectives manning many windows in the towers of the building that overlooked the street and the shops on the other side.

No police vehicle arrived from the police station. What if the criminals got away in the meantime? Swara, hugging her orange knitted doll close, was scared out of her skin (saying, saying!).

Things were definitely going into high gear up in the sari shop. The flashing, dancing lights had moved from the sari shop, very quickly this time, down to the salon below it, then through the wall to the lamp shop, and finally to the ground-floor shop below that—the jewelry shop, shuttered and barred to the street.

Thankfully, before Swara chewed her fingernails and the orange doll's braid off, she heard the rumble of an approaching motorcycle—two regular policemen patrolling on their bike. They were a good enough start.

Rishi, too, seemed visibly relieved. This was his part of the plan. He was to flag down the police patrol when they came along. He jumped around, yelling out incomprehensible warnings through his mask and waving at them from this side of the street. Muffet jumped. Govind Uncle waved.

The policemen on the bike seemed pleased. Helmets on, they probably couldn't hear much, but they were used to people applauding them during this pandemic. They slowed a bit, waved enthusiastically back, and rolled on.

No! Oh no! Swara hopped around. The plan was not going according to plan at all. "Pitter Paati, make them do something," she appealed to the picture, the moon, the stars—just in case.

Rishi did something instead. Something weird. And not very lawful at all. In his defense, however, he had to do something out of the ordinary to get the police to turn their attention back to him. It's called Creative Thinking. And there are a million online courses to learn it, but none that will teach you something like this.

Rishi picked up Muffet and placed him on a long, sleek white car that was parked outside their gate. Muffet, indignant, slid around and then jumped off the car soon enough. But that was sufficient to set the car's alarm screeching, which in turn sent Muffet into a frantic barking fit. Good boy, Little Miss Muffet! Swara grinned.

That put the mission back on track.

The policemen swiveled toward the sound and turned the motorcycle around, not happy anymore. They parked near Rishi and Govind Uncle. The gestures this time told Swara that they had begun to question Rishi, who went on to report the alleged crime. One officer began to cross the street to investigate this teen's strange claims.

Meanwhile, the screeching alarm that was not part of the plan, but just Rishi's V. Creative Thinking, had alerted the ghost-men. Swara, from her vantage point, saw the flashing lights go back the way they'd come—up to the lamp shop, through to the salon, up to the sari shop. In a couple of minutes, the two men emerged from the sari shop's stairwell, bent under bulky sacks thrown over their shoulders, and charged toward their minivan.

It was dark in that particular spot because of the broken streetlamp. The policeman was midway across the street. The police station hadn't sent anyone yet. Swara felt helpless. Stuck at home, solving a crime across the street. What had she been thinking? V. Obviously it was not possible. This only happened in films. The criminals were getting away. They were already throwing their sacks into their van and jumping in.

When she was close to hysterics, another vehicle appeared in the distance, its headlights casting a strong beam before it. It was the police jeep! The local police station had sent officers after all. Zarir's doctor father was a hero!

The police jeep, with a screech of tires, stopped right in the getaway path of the minivan, which was pulling away from its parking spot. Both the policemen from the patrolling motorcycle had run across the street by now, Govind Uncle following, Rishi and Muffet bringing up the rear. So when the two suspects, whose vehicular exit was blocked, jumped out of the van, balancing their sacks, they were easily surrounded by the crime-fighting squad. Swara was thrilled to see that one of the police officers who got out of the jeep was a woman. Fool Rishi would now have to admit that she was correct in drawing that triangular belly.

She was even prouder to see that Muffet behaved just like an awesome super-detective subagent dog. He yapped and ran around in circles—knotting his leash around Rishi's legs and almost bringing him down—peed on the tire of the evil minivan, attacked shadows, tried to chew on one of the sacks, and strangely enough, seemed to frighten the two men, who held their arms up in surrender.

Rishi waved back across the street at their apartment, at his sister in the lit-up window. Swara blinked her light on and off. Eleven lights across other apartments blinked on and off in response.

# The Whole Ruth

Swara was in the news over the next couple of days. In headlines in newspapers, tickers on the local news channel, on a national news channel, on a few news blogs, and on her school's online newsletter.

*EIGHT-YEAR-OLD BUSTS BURGLARY RING*

**ONE SAVED MILLIONS: THE LOCKDOWN HEIST**

**BENGALURU CHILDREN
GET THE GOLD**

She was rather disappointed, though. She had written out an elaborate list of Steps in the Mystery Solving. Pitter Paati's detectives always laid out their steps in the last scene, in a grand revelation of how they solved the crime. However, not a single reporter paid attention long enough.

They were more interested in how old she was (which they got wrong), how much the gold was worth (which she had no clue about), who the thieves were (no clue, no clue), if she could stop talking and smile sweetly for the camera, etc.

Swara had been super excited when reporters called to ask for video chats.

"I have to look fantastic. And smart. Should I wear Rishi's spectacles to look smart? I must give the others credit—and especially Pitter Paati for all the clues. I know—I will wear her sari. No? Okay, then what? Her necklace? No? Why not? My hair is looking V. Rubbish. No, I don't want oil. Should I wear a mask? What clothes should I wear? No, not pink. No, not my uniform. No, I hate those pants, why would you tell me to wear that? No, that one's too shiny, and that dress is too babyish, and white looks too goody-goody. Can I hold PP's picture? No, why not? Can I hold my orange doll?"

Finally, after much persuasion, Swara was made to sit up straight on a dining chair. Amma connected to the video calls while sitting near her. On her own insistence, she wore Pitter Paati's scarf around her neck. She tried to hold Muffet on her lap, which turned out somewhat disastrous. He squiggled and wriggled. He tried to chew the end of the scarf, so she almost suffocated on the national news.

The actual interviews showed only a small clip of a girl with large eyes and hair flying around, clutching a squirming pup. In the middle of the clip, the neighbor's pressure cooker whistle went off, drowning out her words while Muffet freed himself and ran off to attack the offending pressure cooker. They switched to showing the two men with handkerchiefs around their faces.

The news said that a jewelry heist worth millions was stopped by an eight-year-old ("But I kept saying I was almost nine," Swara wailed) and her friends from the buildings across the street. The thief was an ex-manager of the sari shop, which was why he had a duplicate key. The thieves drilled an intricate passageway for themselves, down through the floor of the sari shop to the salon, through the wall to the lamp shop in the adjoining building, and then through

its floor to get to the jewelry shop. They worked at night and in the dark, only occasionally using the lights from their phones. Since the shops around were in lockdown, and the street in front had hardly any traffic and no pedestrians, the sound wasn't noticed at all. A security guard questioned said he'd heard an occasional buzz, but who was he to run after every buzz? The shop owners had not been allowed to enter their shops either. The police patrol had not noticed anything amiss.

Amma-Appa were surprised, proud, and elated, and couldn't stop congratulating themselves at the thought of their young one doing so much from her bedroom window.

"She has my mother's brains," Amma claimed later.

"I got her that puppy," Appa claimed.

"Puppet! That's the name Swara gave him," Rishi said.

"He is Little Miss Muffet!" Swara stamped her foot. But of course, they were all smiling.

☆ ☆ ☆

There was one reporter—it needs to be said—who had the entire proceedings down, every single step.

"This is Ruth of the Matter," she began, training her sister's cell phone on Swara across the hall. "And I have the whole scoop."

"Of what? Where? Vanilla?" Swara looked confused, sitting cross-legged on her mat in her doorway. She was going to give Ruth the real story. Ruth deserved to be part of the glory too. That's what friends are for.

"We are interviewing Swara, a.k.a. Miss Marble, dear viewers. How did you sit at your window and know there was a theft being planned across the street?"

"Firstly, it all started when I was almost four, with the detective stories that—" Swara began.

Ruth leaned out and said in a stage whisper, "Don't go so far back. The phone battery won't last. Start with the flashing lights."

Swara frowned. "Okay. Firstly, there were the flashing lights in the sari shop. Two men were going in there at night and coming out in the morning. But they didn't put on the stair lights or the shop's main lights. And I wondered why. I realized they were only going around with their cell phone lights flashing."

"You did not realize anything. You said they were dancing ghosts, remember?"

"I will not give you the entire report if you keep butting in."

"A good reporter asks the right questions."

"Okay, now be quiet." Swara hurried through in case Ruth slipped in another fool question. "Secondly, passing car headlights kept flashing on and off Pitter Paati's picture, and that made me realize something else. The dancing lights in the sari shop also flashed off at times, and they always, always went off when the police motorcycle was passing or a police van was patrolling. Why?"

"Why? You want me to answer?"

"No. Me. So, the answer is that the people were up to no good, as Thaatha says. They were trying to avoid being seen by the police. V. Exciting but V. Suspicious too. I knew something bad was happening, but I was locked down here. Thirdly, Little Miss Muffet was digging in the mud, which is what made me think of those people digging, and that's how they were going into different shops. They were digging holes through ceilings and walls. I sent Rishi to check."

"Who is Rishi?"

"Huh? You know who Rishi is. What is wrong with you?"

"This is Ruth of the Matter, and nothing is wrong with me. I find out the Ruth at any cost. Who is Rishi for our many dear viewers?"

Swara sulked a bit but bravely carried on. "Rishi is my older brother, who is almost seventeen, and thirdly, he went over to check. He took his phone and dog, my dog, that is, Little Miss Muffet, across the street. To get eye drops from the pharmacy, which was closed."

"Then how could he get eye drops?"

"He couldn't."

"You said he got eye drops. That is not the whole Ruth; that is a lie."

"Stop and listen. *You* need *ear* drops. I said he went to get them, not that he got them. Anyway, so thirdly—"

"You said thirdly thrice."

"I will go give someone else my scoop if you go on like this, Ruth! Thirdly, he strolled over to the stairway leading up to the sari shop to check if there were any untoward sounds, and he heard the hammering and drilling coming from upstairs. Proof at last! Wasn't so loud, but he heard it. And he recorded it too. So there!"

"Where?"

"It's a saying."

"They could have been repairing something. People drill and hammer when they repair. The people in the building are always complaining about that."

"That is why you are not a detective and I am. Now, fifthly—"

"You didn't say fourthly . . ."

"I did."

"You didn't."

"Okay, fourthly, then. Once we confirmed my suspicions, then Pitter Paati helped out. I knew they were drilling and making a hole, but I thought it was to steal saris and escape."

"Why couldn't they steal saris and escape the way they got in? Through the stairs, since the sari shop ex-manager had the key?" Ruth tilted her camera toward herself, mighty pleased with her own questions.

Swara scowled. "I didn't say they were stealing saris. I said I thought they were . . . Listen and stop confusing me. So fourthly, I was dressing up as Pitter

Paati to be like her. And then Amma said one thing was missing and she put a gold chain on me. And as I stared at the mirror, it hit me."

"The mirror hit you? Or Pitter Paati from the mirror hit you? Or the gold necklace hit you, or your Amma hit you?"

Swara ignored her V. Annoyingness. "The truth hit me. I knew why and where they were drilling. They were making holes in the walls and floors to get to the ground-floor shop in the next building. The gold jewelry shop. Because that's what the gold necklace reminded me of. Gold! The main reason they were doing all this criminal stuff. I knew then why the lights were flashing around, sometimes up, sometimes in the salon below, sometimes in the lamp shop next to it. Their final destination was the gold shop, but they couldn't get in there directly without being seen from the street, and the gold shop has so many shutters and locks and all. Only way in was a hole through the ceiling!"

Ruth leaned forward. "That is brilliant deduction, Swara! Wow!"

"Wait, it's not over. Fifthly . . ." Swara consulted

her notes. "Yes, the fifth step was to prove this crime was going to happen. No one would believe us kids, remember? So that's why I organized the night watch to catch the criminals red-handed. All of us kids kept awake in shifts all through the night, keeping watch on the opposite side of the street to report any untoward event."

"Except me. I was not included. Because my apartment is untoward," Ruth grumbled. "Go on to the sixth step quickly now, this step is boring."

"Sixthly, I guessed that the criminals would plan a special something to actually take their haul of gold away. I mean, they only came in with small backpacks to maybe carry drills or screwdrivers or whatever. And on a motorbike. So we would notice if they changed their modus operandi," Swara ended with a flourish. She had checked this phrase and practiced it in front of the mirror. It sounded every bit as awesome as she thought it would.

Ruth seemed impressed too. "And then, Swara, er, Miss Marble, how did you catch them?" She leaned out. "It's going on too long. End it now."

"Okay, okay, so sixthly, seventhly, whatever . . .

when Uttara saw the minivan that night, I knew they were going to make their move. Then we put the rest of the plan into action. The seventh step was Zarir calling his doctor father to tell the local police station to send a police team so they could catch the criminals. But that took so long. So eighthly, Rishi took Little Miss Muffet down again, and he and Govind Uncle stopped the police motorcycle by setting off a car alarm. And that was where Muffet played his role—please make sure that you give him credit. And then—okay, okay." She noticed Ruth slicing her finger across her own throat in a sign to kill the report quickly. "Then, the criminals came rushing down with their sacks of gold, and—"

"And that, my dear viewers, is the Ruth, the whole Ruth, and nothing but the Ruth."

"And the Swara!"

"Yes, the Ruth and the Swara. I hope that recorded all right, or we will have to do the whole painful thing again. This time we can ask Rishi. We only have to say Debbie is asking, and hehe . . . Oh, oh no, it's still recording. Off, off!"

The video interview did the rounds on the

apartment complex chat group the next day, and neighbors called in with plenty of good things to say: congratulations, and how they knew that Swara was brilliant, and the kids were such smart and wonderful little citizens full of talent and potential—and all that. The apartment committee promised the kids a big party as soon as the lockdown was lifted, and as soon as big parties were allowed once more.

# From Black to Gold

The sun smiled in through Swara's curtains, painting the room in gold.

It was the day she turned nine. Finally. A V. Huge leap, you'll agree, from almost nine to nine. And from the next day onward, she'd start counting herself as almost ten.

There were no gifts because no one could go out to get them. That wasn't really important. She'd gotten Little Miss Muffet, after all, and that made up for years ahead without gifts. However, her morning was filled with plenty of calls, wishes, virtual hugs, kisses, blessings. She didn't get the V. Precious one that usually woke her up. She went instead to PP's framed photograph on the wall and gave it a V. Long kiss. She was even allowed to take Muffet out all on her own. A V. Responsible thing for a V. Responsible nine-year-old.

Amma-Appa and Rishi spent the morning in the kitchen. They were cooking up a storm, and they wouldn't even let her in to taste. Being an exceptional detective, she could tell from the different aromas wafting out of the kitchen what exactly was being cooked, and she totally approved. She thought she'd do her bit. She cleaned Muffet's bowls and filled one with fresh water. She laid out the table mats and the usual steel plates and steel tumblers on the table. She filled the water jug. She laid out the jute runner in the middle so that the hot dishes could be placed on it.

Amma said, "Lovely, Swara, thank you. Would you mind changing the plates, though?"

"Huh?" After all her hard work! Grown-ups! V. Weird!

Amma opened the glass-paned cabinet on the wall and very carefully lifted out the white plates from the top shelf. The plates that had fine gold rims and delicate gold leaves running across those rims. The plates that were only taken out on special occasions, like when guests came over for dinner. The plates that on usual days, everyone could look at and admire in the cabinet but not eat off. Because—what if they broke by accident?

"The do-not-touch plates?" Swara asked, eyes wide. "The what-if-they-break plates?"

"The special-occasion plates, because this is a special occasion." Amma placed the last plate carefully on the table. "You can even go wash them yourself. One by one."

"I can touch the do-not-touch plates? Why?" Swara did not want to fall into a trap.

"Because, kitty-kutty, this lockdown has taught us all that there is no point in keeping things locked away for some grand future, because we don't know what the future will be. Humans don't know everything."

"Dogs do?"

"I don't know. You'll have to ask Muffet that. But I know some things, like your Pitter Paati would have wanted you to have the best today. And I agree, because you deserve the best. We all do, Swara. There's no point in keeping our finest plates away—we need to enjoy them ourselves."

Mentioning PP reminded Swara of what she had planned to do. She took the scarf she'd knitted for Pitter Paati and wrapped it around the fifth chair at the head of the table, and over lunch, they talked about Pitter Paati whenever they felt like it, without holding anything back, not memories, not tears, not giggles, not jokes.

Muffet was also treated to a little bit of everything they'd cooked, even though the vet had recommended that he get special dog food only. He didn't seem to mind. He licked his lips and stared at them with puppy eyes. Appa gave him a second helping. Rishi gave him a third.

Needless to say (or perhaps it's needed, since we keep so many things unsaid), they had an absolutely fabulous meal, for which Rishi took most of the credit. He'd made a very special rice pudding for Swara.

"Rishi, it's just like the one Pitter Paati made for me. It's her recipe? The extra-sweet one?"

"It is, Boondi."

"Thanks, Rishi," she said quickly, to reclaim her reputation for exceptional manners in Appa's eyes. "And thank you for not putting curry leaves in."

☆ ☆ ☆

Swara waddled, her stomach very full after that lunch, over to the kitchen, where she helped wash the special-occasion-and-this-was-the-most-special plates. Then she did something quite strange.

She unwrapped the scarf from the chair and walked over to the balcony.

It was a blustery, windy, chilly-though-sunny day, the kind Bengaluru blesses its people with quite often. She leaned over the balcony and called out to their security guard standing downstairs.

"Govind Uncle! Govind Uncle, today's my birthday. I am now nine years old."

The old man, who'd seen Swara from the day she was born, waved gleefully up at her. "God bless you, Baby. Happy birthday, happy birthday, Baby! I have no present for you now."

"I have a present for you, Govind Uncle." Swara swung the scarf out with a swish and waved it at him.

He nodded. "It is so pretty, Baby. And it has been so cold these days."

Swara said proudly, "I knitted it myself. And I will be very V. Happy if you wear it."

The scarf glittered in all its multicolored grandeur, pink, orange, yellow, purple, and—as the sun that slid out from behind the clouds caught it—a glint of gold. And then, she let it go.

She let go.

# Acknowledgments

op of this list is my editor, Susan Kochan, whose sagacity and commitment made Impossible Happen. The story stands stronger because of her, and it makes me wonder why editors' names don't go on the cover. The book you hold owes its journey to the incredible team at Penguin (USA), in particular to Jen Klonsky, publisher, whose warm welcome was a shot in the arm; Matt Phipps; Natalie Vielkind, Emily Rodriguez, and Madison Penico; Cindy Howle and Ana Deboo; Cecilia Yung and Eileen Savage; Amy White; Alex Deguise; and Shanta Newlin, Emily Romero, Alex Garber, Deborah Polansky, and their teams. Thank you to Sofia Pereira. The best Singapore laksa on this island awaits you all.

Many thanks to Mita Kapur, literary agent and

wand-waver. To Sohini Mitra, Arpita Nath, and Akangksha Sarmah from Penguin Random House India. To Jehanzeb Baldiwala for the psychologist perspective. To the warm, wonderful circle of book people: author friends, literature fest organizers, bookstores, reading groups, interviewers, and reviewers, and to the readers whose reviews keep me writing. And as always, to Suroop, Neel, and Nikash for making my happy news their own.

I remember, with gratitude, Aditi Batra, first editor of the first manuscript, who will see the journey it's making from somewhere beyond Swara's moon.

## This Book Is Because . . .

When my boys lost their grandmother, I went about it all wrong. I buried my own feelings and distracted theirs in a frantic rush to face the world as normal, to return to them what I perceived as their required state of equilibrium. I messed up. Over the years, I have delved deeper into better ways of healing. This book comes from that personal space. It is a look at loss through the uncomprehending eyes of children, to let them know it is okay; no one can take the blame and no one can make the pain go away, yet it slowly will.

"Being there" is what you can do for someone going through a dark time. For me, it was my husband, my extended family, our second family at D306, and a few very, very special friends.

**JANE DE SUZA** is the author of several best-selling books published in India. She writes a humor column for *The Hindu*, a daily newspaper in India, and had a parenting column for *Good Housekeeping*. Jane earned an MBA at the Xavier School of Management in Jamshedpur, India, and has worked in advertising for many years as a creative director. She currently lives in Singapore with her family.